FALSELY ACCUSED

"These charges are untrue," Lady Appleton said. "Why were they made against you?"

"You believe me?" Her face betraying both confusion and relief, Mistress Crane slumped against the wall. Her brief spurt of defiance seemed to have used up all her strength. "I do not know why," she insisted. "I do not understand any of what happened to us."

"You must not give up hope, Constance. If you say there was no witchcraft involved, then I believe you, and I will do all I can to help you prove it. The first thing we must do is find another way to account for the deaths. If we can prove someone else murdered those people and explain why, the authorities must perforce set you free."

"Why do you care? You have no reason to help me and every excuse to continue to leave me here to rot." Her eyes narrowed. "What do you gain by appearing here now?"

"Justice," Lady Appleton said simply. "Justice."

Books by Kathy Lynn Emerson

FACE DOWN IN THE MARROW-BONE PIE
FACE DOWN UPON AN HERBAL
FACE DOWN AMONG THE WINCHESTER GEESE
FACE DOWN BENEATH THE ELEANOR CROSS
FACE DOWN UNDER THE WYCH ELM

Published by Kensington Books

FACE DOWN UNDER THE WYCH ELM

Kathy Lynn Emerson

KENSINGTON BOOKS
Kensington Publishing Corp.
http://www.kensingtonbooks.com

KENSINGTON BOOKS are published by

Kensington Publishing Corp.
850 Third Avenue
New York, NY 10022

All Kensington Titles, Imprints, and Distributed Lines are
available at special quantity discounts for bulk purchases for
sales promotions, premiums, fund-raising, educational, or in-
stitutional use. Special book excerpts or customized print-
ings can also be created to fit specific needs. For details,
write or phone the office of the Kensington special sales
manager: Kensington Publishing Corp., 850 Third Avenue,
New York, NY 10022, attn: Special Sales Department,
Phone: 1-800-221-2647.

First Printing: May 2002
10 9 8 7 6 5 4 3 2 1

Printed in the United States of America

1

Her way illuminated by a full moon, Constance Crane left Mill Hall in the hour before midnight to follow the footpath that led past the abandoned chapel. The unexpected crack of a twig under her own foot made her gasp. Closing her eyes for a moment, she waited for her heart to stop racing. She told herself there was nothing to fear. She had walked the short distance to her cousin's cottage many times in daylight. She ought to be able to navigate the route blindfolded.

As she resumed her journey, her wary gaze attracted by every flicker of movement, every wisp of sound, she wondered if having her eyes covered might not be an advantage.

Shimmering moonlight picked out the most hazardous obstacles underfoot—exposed roots and rocks and the like—and helped her stay on the hard-packed trail, but it also created ominous shadows. Constance had the uneasy sense someone was behind her, keeping just out of sight but watching her every move.

Nonsense! Who would be abroad at this hour? There were more reasons to remain within doors than to go

out. Sensible folk went to bed early and rose with the
sun to take up the day's duties. Constance doubted
she'd be able to perform with her accustomed efficiency on the morrow, thanks to this night's business,
but that could not be helped. Nor would she change
her mind about meeting Lucy. Constance had promised to assist her cousin, and she prided herself on
being a woman of her word.

She hurried past the chapel and the two giant elms
that stood on either side of it like twin sentinels. Had
they been planted there to guard a holy place against
evil? Superstition held that spirits walked the earth after dark. Demons appeared then, too, and the faeries
who made the milk go sour. And everyone knew that
corruption traveled in the night air, spreading the
plague and other terrible sicknesses.

Dread riding on her shoulder, Constance had to
force herself to plunge into the thick cluster of trees
beyond the chapel. Why had she never realized how
closely packed they were? Above her head, interwoven
branches of elm and beech stood out in silhouette
against the sky, swaying and dipping in a strange dance
choreographed by gusts of wind coming in off the Narrow Seas.

A low-growing bush snagged Constance's skirt. She
broke into a run, certain it was a hand grasping at her.
A moment later, she burst free of the wooded stretch,
entering the rectangular clearing that was her goal. By
then, her chest heaved and her heart seemed to slam
against her ribs with every ragged breath.

Lucy waited outside her door, a basket over one arm.
She regarded Constance's panic-stricken countenance
and harried demeanor with ill-concealed amusement.
"I perceive you have never been out alone in the dark
before. There is naught to fear from traveling by night,

but it might have been less upsetting had you carried a lantern."

Brought up short by the brusque, matter-of-fact words, Constance reined in her overactive imagination and felt herself flush with embarrassment even as she grew calmer. She could not deny she was relieved to have reached the cottage, but when she looked over her shoulder she saw that Lucy was right. She'd had no reason to be frightened. Neither man nor demon nor faery king had followed her out of the trees.

Only a ghost, she thought with wry self-mockery.

For this was not, in truth, the first time she had braved the night's dangers on her own. Her memory jogged by Lucy's comment, Constance recalled with vivid clarity that long-ago midnight when she'd crept out of the room where Lady Northampton's ladies slept and gone to meet a lover. She'd been very young and surpassing foolish, and she'd had no qualms about braving the extensive gardens of a country estate in the dark to give herself to a handsome young man in the duke of Northumberland's household. Together they'd reveled in the heady delights of the flesh and in the excitement of their own daring.

"Come along," Lucy urged, taking Constance's arm for support. She hobbled a bit, lame in one leg, but she made good speed. Constance had to move swiftly to keep pace with her.

Lucy's excitement was so intense that she fair vibrated with it. There was no stopping her. After being bedridden and housebound for much of the winter just past, she was determined upon her quest.

Constance was prepared to endure for Lucy's sake. Although she knew a number of people who had lived more than her cousin's sixty years, they were hardy souls. Lucy was frail, unfit to go wandering through the woods alone. And yet, if Constance had not agreed to accompany her, she'd have attempted this expedition on her own. After nursing Lucy all those months, and comforting her more recently, when she'd learned of the death of a longtime acquaintance, Constance felt an obligation to continue looking after her cousin.

Besides, she'd grown fond of Lucy.

Once more, Constance found herself following a moonlit path through thickly wooded darkness. She swallowed an anxious protest when Lucy veered off into the trees. Bereft of all sense of direction, unable to tell if they were still on Mill Hall land or if they had crossed over onto property belonging to the Edgecumbes, Constance put her faith in her cousin. Lucy had confidence enough for them both.

The older woman never faltered, never slowed down until they reached their destination. "There." Triumph in her voice, she pointed one gnarled finger toward a cluster of plants growing wild in the wood.

"I do not see why we could not have come here in daylight," Constance murmured.

"I have told you my reasons." Lucy's querulous voice sounded loud in the stillness of the night. "The leaves are most potent if they are gathered between Lady Day and Midsummer's Eve. Collecting them in the full of the moon adds to their power. Should congestion of the lungs ever bring me as close to death's door again as it did on St. Valentine's Day, then these leaves, plucked at their strongest, have the power to bring back my breath."

Constance had seen for herself how a pinch of this herb, ground and dissolved in sweet wine, had eased Lucy's struggle to breathe. Besides, they were here now. They might as well continue. She picked her way over the last uneven stretch, knelt, and reached for the nearest stalk.

"Wait!"

With excruciating slowness, Lucy lowered herself to the ground beside Constance. One knee made a sharp popping sound.

"Ritual is important. The herb must be crossed and blessed when it is gathered." She made the sign of the cross, then bowed her head. "Hallowed be thou, vervain, as thou growest in the ground, for in the mount of Calvary, there thou was first found. Thou healedst our Saviour, Jesus Christ, and staunchedst his bleeding wound. In the name of the Father, the Son, and the Holy Ghost, I take thee from the ground."

No hasty plucking of leaves would do for Lucy Milborne. Constance resigned herself to following her cousin's exacting instructions. There were more prayers when the job was done. By then, Lucy's bad leg had further stiffened from kneeling in the early-morning dew. They returned to her cottage at a snail's pace. Dawn was not far off when they reached the door of the stillroom.

"I have one other favor to ask of you, child." Lucy deposited her basket, filled to overflowing, on a long worktable.

Tired as she was, Constance did not think of refusing. She even managed a small smile at her cousin's use of the endearment. Lucy might be some twenty years older than she, but by no stretch of the imagination did that make Constance a child.

"There is a root in my herb garden that needs digging up." Lucy rubbed her right knee. "I can do the work myself. Never think I cannot. But without your help I will have the devil's own time getting to my feet again when it is done."

"I will unearth your root for you, Lucy. Only tell me which one it is." Constance had lived so long in the household of the late marchioness of Northampton, without making use of her early lessons in plant lore, that she had all but forgotten them. She knew the smells and uses of more apothecary-made medicines than most women but was perilous ignorant when it came to the appearance of single ingredients in their natural state.

The rising sun found Lucy and Constance both kneeling in Lucy's small garden. What should have been a simple task had taken far longer than either of them had anticipated. Constance glanced up from her struggles to discover she'd been caught in a most undignified position by one of the servants from Mill Hall. Arthur Kennison was gaping at them from the path. When she scowled at him, he hastened to avert his eyes and continue on his way through the clearing.

Lucy gave a dismissive snort. "That fellow again!"

"Does he often come this way?"

"Of late he does."

Constance stared in puzzlement after the rapidly disappearing figure. That path, if one stayed on it instead of veering off to pick vervain, led to only one place—Edgecumbe Manor.

"Is he on his own business or Hugo's?" Constance wondered aloud.

Hugo Garrard, who was cousin to both Lucy and herself, had spent considerable time with his nearest neighbor before Clement Edgecumbe's sudden death. He might well make a special effort to look out for Edgecumbe's widow and daughter, but would he choose to send Kennison, the least trustworthy of Mill Hall's servants, to carry his messages?

"Help me up," Lucy said, distracting Constance from her speculations.

When she'd settled her cousin in the stillroom, Constance returned to Mill Hall. The way was passing ordinary in daylight.

Busy with her duties as Hugo's housekeeper, Constance had no notion that anything was amiss in the neighborhood until the local constable, a carpenter by trade, arrived late in the day.

"I are come to arrest you, Mistress Crane."

At first, her amazement tempered any feeling of apprehension. His words made no sense. Neither did the emotion she recognized in his eyes. Why should he be afraid?

"For what crime?"

"It is charged that you and old Mother Milborne did bewitch Peter Marsh to death and that she did kill Clement Edgecumbe by witchcraft."

Stunned, Constance took a step away from him. She could scarce take in all the shocks contained in that one sentence. For a moment, she fixed on the least of the strangeness, wondering why he'd addressed Lucy as Mother instead of Mistress.

Then the rest of what he'd said crashed in on her. A ripple of alarm shook her out of her state of dazed incomprehension.

"Marsh cannot be dead." Constance had seen Hugo's former clerk only two days earlier. He'd been hale and hearty . . . and up to his usual tricks.

Hugo, face pale within a shock of reddish brown hair and the little tuft of his beard, his heavy-lidded eyes wider than Constance had ever seen them, came up behind the constable. Arthur Kennison, stone-faced and for once showing no evidence of being cup-shot, appeared at his elbow.

" 'Tis true, Constance," Hugo said. "I can scarce believe it myself, but we have just been to see the body. There is no doubt it is Marsh."

Death could come of a sudden. She knew that. But accepting Marsh's demise forced her to contemplate the remainder of the constable's remarkable statement. Her hands felt clammy as she clenched them into fists at her sides. Holding herself still, she struggled to order her thoughts and keep panic at bay.

Marsh was dead and she was accused of killing him. By witchcraft.

"I am not a witch," she whispered.

"How else do you explain the circumstances of his death?"

Drawn by the commotion, Mill Hall's servants had left their duties to come and gawk at the tableau in the hall. The cook, who just an hour earlier had exchanged cheerful, friendly words with Constance, now shrank from her in revulsion. Emma, the young maidservant she'd befriended, appeared to be too terrified to speak. And the chaplain, who might have been expected to play a role in such proceedings, kept in the background, his expression guarded.

"When did he die?" Constance managed to conquer her dread long enough to address the constable. "And where?"

"He was found this morning, within sight of Mother Milborne's cottage." The constable lowered his voice as a note of awe crept into it. "He lay dead, not a mark upon him, face down under the wych elm."

In the horrified silence that followed this announcement, Constance began to feel light-headed. Her stomach clenched in fear.

"Mother Milborne is already in custody," the constable continued. "You will both be tooken to Maidstone for trial at the summer Assizes."

Maidstone—the shire town for Kent.

Assizes—the twice-annual court at which felons were tried. And after, executed.

Constance fought for control of her reeling senses. She must not scream or faint. She had to think. There must be some way out of this terrifying situation.

She was not a witch and neither was Lucy.

Lucy was accused of bewitching Clement Edgecumbe to death? Had the constable said that? The charge was preposterous. Lucy had still been all but bedridden when her neighbor died. And she'd been distraught when the news was brought to her that he was dead. They'd not been friends. They'd quarreled too often for that. But they'd known each other all their lives and Lucy had admitted to Constance that she'd miss "the old goat."

Constance tried again to deny the charges, but no one listened. Under guard, she was escorted to her own bedchamber. She and Lucy, she was informed, were to be kept prisoner at Mill Hall overnight and taken north on the morrow. There was a proper gaol in Maidstone.

Left alone, Constance could no longer hold her horror at bay. She sat, staring at nothing, and let it wash over her in crashing waves. But she had never been the sort to weep and wail and bemoan her fate. When the onslaught had at last passed by, she was able to think again, to consider what she could do to save herself.

If Lucy had been fit, Constance would have found her, freed her, and run away, but that was not possible.

The Assizes, she remembered, met sometime in the middle of July. That meant she and Lucy would spend many weeks in gaol. She did not allow herself to dwell on that bleak prospect but instead considered that the same span of time might be used to their benefit. They'd need an ally, someone she could persuade to look into the two deaths and discover their true cause.

An ironic smile twisted Constance's lips at the name that came at once to mind. Yes, she would know how to proceed. She had been in a similar situation herself some two years earlier. She'd escaped the gallows by uncovering the identity of the real murderer.

She was also the last person on earth who would be inclined to help Constance Crane, for she was the widow of the man Constance had met in that garden, and other gardens, all those years ago.

Constance passed a long, sleepless night but she could think of no one better suited to her purpose. She spent the hour before dawn composing a letter. She had nothing to lose by asking, and she did not make her request only for herself. Lucy had never even met Constance's lover.

"Thank the Lord," Constance whispered when the first person to enter her chamber was someone she considered trustworthy.

In haste, before the constable and his men came to take her away, she explained what she wanted done.

She left Mill Hall buoyed up by a faint stirring of hope. She'd exacted a promise. Within the hour, a messenger would be dispatched to take her missive to its destination.

2

The outside of the folded page had been inscribed with six words. An irritated voice read them aloud.

"Susanna, Lady Appleton. Leigh Abbey, Kent." The name was unfamiliar to the person who now had possession of Constance's letter. Gloved fingers broke the seal. Angry eyes skimmed over the words Constance had written.

The crackle of parchment being crumpled into a ball sounded loud in an otherwise silent chamber.

This would not do. Whoever this Lady Appleton was, she could not be permitted to meddle. She must never even learn Constance had attempted to contact her.

The hands that tore the letter to bits and then thrust the pieces into a candle flame shook a little, not in trepidation but with suppressed fury. How dare Constance try to escape her fate? Everything that had been done would be for naught if she could prove herself and Lucy innocent. The two women who had been accused of witchcraft must be convicted and executed.

By the time the last bit of parchment had been reduced to ash, the tip of one gloved finger had been singed. Its owner did not notice.

Deep satisfaction slowly began to replace the rage.

3

On a warm, sunny morning, Nick Baldwin followed the narrow, deeply worn track that ran between his home, Whitethorn Manor, and neighboring Leigh Abbey. In recent months he'd made frequent use of this shortcut between the two estates.

It emerged from the woods just at the edge of Leigh Abbey's apple orchards. Nick passed through rows of costards, which made good cider and good eating, and continued on past long, pear-shaped pearmains and both summer and russet pippins before coming to a perimeter of pear and cherry trees. At that point, the path became a gravel walkway leading up a little rise.

Susanna Appleton waited at the top, watching him approach in much the same manner she had the first time they'd met. Nick's remembering smile contained an element of wry, self-mocking humor. Back then, he'd expected Lady Appleton to be a common-variety country gentlewoman, more interested in cultivating strawberries the size of hedge blackberries than in matters beyond the domestic realm.

How wrong he'd been! She was indeed diligent about her gardening, and she had made of Leigh Abbey a profitable estate, but she also wrote books and meddled in political matters and had accumulated the oddest assortment of friends and acquaintances anyone could imagine.

She stood as he crested the knoll, greeting him with an affectionate kiss. He was a trifle shorter than she, but then Susanna was uncommon tall for a woman. She'd once told him she took after her father, inheriting his height, his sturdy build, and his square jaw, as well as his love of learning. Nick had long since decided that none of those attributes detracted from her feminine appeal. She was as captivating as she was unique and the intricate workings of her mind had fascinated him from the first.

"Come and sit beside me," she invited, resuming her place on the stone bench and making room for him by holding aside the folds of her black damask kirtle.

Susanna was a widow. A strict traditionalist would insist she wear naught but black for the rest of her life, or until she remarried, but Susanna was not such a hypocrite. She did not mourn the loss of her husband enough to put off dressing in bright colors forever. Only the fact that she was frugal by nature kept her wearing those widow's weeds which had not yet worn out. To the black silk bodice that matched her kirtle she had fastened bright green sleeves embroidered with yellow and red butterflies.

"Can it be nearly five years since we first met?" Nick took the seat she offered. They had a degree of privacy seated there, shaded by the low-hanging branches of an ancient elm, but he had no doubt that most of Susanna's servants already knew he had arrived.

"Time passes with more speed than we realize, my dear." A mischievous glint came into her eyes. "But I remember that particular occasion as if it were yesterday. Every detail."

"I was in error. I hasten to admit it."

The reason behind his initial visit to Leigh Abbey still had the power to make Nick squirm, He'd accused one of Susanna's servants of theft. She'd reacted by insisting she be allowed to conduct her own investigation of the crime. It had not taken her long to discover the identity of the real thief. She'd won Nick's grudging admiration in the process. Before long, she had also captured his heart.

From their vantage point they had a fine, panoramic view. On the one hand were the orchards and the woods through which Nick had just come. On the other were Leigh Abbey's extensive gardens and the house itself.

"The plums will be ripe in another month." Susanna nodded toward the semicircular space just below their little knoll. A combination of shrubs, flowers, and fruit trees flourished there. "And the apricots, if all goes well, will produce their first crop for me in August."

They shared an interest in horticulture, among other things. In his travels, Nick had encountered all manner of unusual plants. He had introduced Susanna to his favorite spice, one he'd taken a liking to during a visit to Persia. Turmeric, it was called. It came from India.

Over the last few years, once he learned how much Susanna delighted in discovering which plants would grow in England's soil and climate and which could only be cultivated in their native habitats, he'd begun to import rare seeds and cuttings for her. The turmeric had failed to prosper, needing a warmer, wetter place in which to thrive, but Susanna had high hopes for a thornapple seedling for which Nick had sent all the way to Constantinople.

Capturing one of Susanna's hands, he waited until she met his eyes. "I will not be here to see the apricots,

Susanna. Nor the barberries or filberts or muskmelons or pears."

Alarmed, she tightened her grip on his fingers. "Are you ill, Nick?"

Her concern pleased him. Gave him hope. He shook his head. "I must go away for a time."

"To London?"

"To Hamburg."

She blinked at him in surprise.

"The city of Hamburg is on the brink of granting the Merchant Adventurers a charter with wide privileges to settle and trade there. It is poised to become the principal gateway for the export of cloth and the import of timber and naval stores. At last, we English will no longer be dependent upon Antwerp for our prosperity."

He did not need to explain further. Susanna knew that a healthy economy required markets and that, with the recent religious and political turmoil in the Low Countries, merchants like Nick were in desperate need of alternate ports on the Continent.

"Hamburg," she murmured. "But must you journey there in person?"

"Aye. I think it best." He turned to face her more fully on the hard stone seat. "I may be gone for some time. Perhaps a year. Perhaps longer."

"I will miss you."

"You might come with me. As my wife."

There. It was out. Nick held his breath and watched her expressive face for a reaction.

She was not a beautiful woman, but Susanna Appleton's features had character. Dark, unruly hair, which always seemed to be escaping from beneath her caps, surrounded a face dominated by intelligent blue eyes. They widened slightly at his words. Her mouth opened, then closed again. Carefully, she withdrew her fingers from his.

"I will never remarry."

Susanna's reply did not surprise Nick, but neither could he contain the brief burst of resentment he felt at her refusal. She claimed to care for him, yet she would not trust him.

Tamping down the spurt of irritation, he reminded himself that she stood to lose a great deal by marrying again. A wife's person, as well as all her possessions, belonged by law to any man who became her husband. Susanna had endured an unhappy marriage for many years and treasured the freedom she had gained as a widow. These days she made all her own decisions.

Nick struggled to sound reasonable. "There is more between us than friendship, Susanna. You know that I—"

"I know that I will not change my mind, Nick. Not even for you."

"We are . . . well suited."

A faint wash of color stained her cheeks, pleasing him beyond measure. "I am honest enough to admit that. If I were willing to marry again, Nick, I can think of no one I'd prefer to you, but marriage is not for me."

And without marriage, he could not with honor take her with him into a foreign land. He'd tried to imagine her living openly as his mistress, but a life of deceit, hiding their true relationship by pretending she was his housekeeper or his sister, would go against her nature.

"When do you leave?" she asked.

How could she sound so calm? Nick tried to match her tone. "My presence is required in Maidstone for the summer Assizes." He noticed her startled look and hastened to explain that he'd not been charged with any crime. "I have a civil case before the justices. Once they render their decision, there will be no further need for me to remain in England."

Noting the preoccupied expression on Susanna's face, he once more turned to contemplate the landscape below. If she would not agree to marry him, there was an end to it.

He scowled at the nearest part of the garden, which was full of plum and apricot trees as well as flowers. It gave way to another laid out in eighteen parallel beds planted with vegetables. Nick had come to know Susanna's crops almost as well as she did. He could pick out sections planted with onions, garlic, leeks, and shallots, and see where they vied for space with beans and pease, sorrel, lettuce, turnips, and skirrets. There were other crops, too, everything from carrots, endive, and cress, to fennel, parsley, chervil, coriander, and dill.

Closer to the house, tucked in between Susanna's stillroom and the kitchen wing, was the physic garden. Roses and lilies bloomed there for color, but most of the space was given over to healing herbs. Just as Susanna had learned the names of Nick's ships, what cargoes they carried and what ports they visited, he could rattle off the names of the most common medicinal plants. Just as she knew that wool and fells from the sheep he raised on his lands in Northamptonshire were carried by cart every spring and autumn to the clothiers in Kent to be made into broadcloth and, more recently, what were called the new draperies, he was able to list the ingredients in a dozen of Susanna's favorite remedies.

They had, he reckoned, spent hundreds of hours together since Sir Robert Appleton's death. She had grieved with him when his old cat, Bala, died. She had helped him deal with the local folk, many of whom still regarded him as an outsider, calling him the London Man behind his back.

"Nick," Susanna said softly, interrupting his ruminations, "it has been some time since I visited Maidstone."

His heart leapt.

"Did you not tell me that you sought a new tenant for the house you own there?"

"Aye. At present it stands empty." Did she mean what he thought she did?

"If Jennet accompanied me, my staying there with you would raise no eyebrows."

"But will your Jennet agree to come? She does not approve of me and I cannot claim to be easy with her, either." Susanna's housekeeper had a mind of her own and a tongue sharp as a rapier. And it had been Jennet whom Nick had wrongly accused of theft.

Susanna's eyes gleamed with mischief. "If not Jennet, then mayhap we can ask your mother to accompany us."

"Given that choice, I will delight in Jennet's presence." With a rueful chuckle, he leaned forward to drop a light kiss on Susanna's smiling lips. Bad enough, he thought, that he was obliged to put up with his mother's presence at Whitethorn Manor.

4

"That woman will be the ruin of him," Winifred Baldwin muttered as she searched her son's belongings.

Nick was there again. At Leigh Abbey. With her.

Winifred made a harrumphing sound as she finished pawing through the contents of a sea chest. Still grumbling, she let the lid slam closed on Nick's clothing and surveyed his chamber for potential hiding places. She knew what she sought, even though she was uncertain what precise form it might take. The Appleton woman had put a spell on Nick. Nothing else could explain his slavish devotion to her, his defiance of his own mother's advice. If there was a love charm hidden in the house, like the one Winifred herself had used to entrap Nick's father almost forty years earlier, she intended to find it.

As in all the rooms at Whitethorn Manor, carpet from Antwerp instead of rushes covered the floor of Nick's bedchamber. He'd acquired some peculiar habits during his sojourn in Persia. Here the rug was green, an oblong four ells long and two ells broad. Most extravagant. What was wrong with rushes, she'd like to know? Or good woven mats of English manufacture?

Winifred stared at the heavy fabric. Was there a hiding place in the floor beneath? If so, it must wait for discovery. Her back ached from her earlier efforts. At present, lifting such a heavy object without assistance was beyond her powers.

Turning her attention to the bed, she recalled that Nick had imported six feather ticks from Brussels the previous year. One lay here, atop his thick, wool-stuffed mattress. Had he given another to her? No doubt he had, along with a sampling of the delicacies made by Antwerp's most skilled confectioners. Winifred had seen a copy of the letter ordering those, but nary a sign of the treats themselves. Her mouth watered as she imagined the delightful tastes—green ginger, white sugar candy, and assorted comfits. Her favorite sweets were almonds dipped in honey.

Winifred turned expert hands to an examination of the layers of fabric covering Nick's bed. He'd hidden nothing under the tapestry coverlet or the down-filled pillows. Her search beneath the blanket of white Spanish felt yielded only a quilt, a second blanket of fustian, and a pair of sheets.

Exasperated, she turned next to the corner of the room hidden by a screen painted in bright colors. Once behind it, she could not hear the sound of soft footfalls on the stairs. She had no inkling that Nick had come into the bedchamber, or stood watching her increasingly frantic search, until he spoke.

"Looking for something, Mother?"

Caught in an undignified crouch beside the close stool, Winifred took a moment to regain her composure before she straightened and turned to face her son. She produced the stub of a candle from her apron pocket, pretending she'd just dropped it. "The wicks needed trimming."

"In the daytime?"

"Harrumph! The light is fading as we speak. 'Twill be dark soon."

"Mother, this has to stop." He caught her arm to help her to her feet and kept hold of her, his grip gentle but unyielding, when she would have barged past him out of the room.

"I have no notion what you mean."

"You understand me very well."

"By St. Frideswide's girdle, I do not understand you at all!"

She, who had spent decades in London trying to ignore her own country origins, could not comprehend Nick's desire to rusticate in this backwater. She could not put all the blame on Lady Appleton, either, no matter how much she wished to do so. Nick had purchased Whitethorn Manor before he'd ever met the woman.

Nick released her, removed his stylish feathered bonnet, and raked agitated fingers through a shock of dark brown hair. There were a few strands of white in it, Winifred noticed, though he was scarce five and thirty. In that, he reminded her of Bevis.

Every hair on her late husband's head had changed color by the time he passed his fortieth birthday. Otherwise, though, Nick took after the men on her side of the family—stocky, but not fat, with broad shoulders. No one would ever call him handsome, but he was not ill-favored, either, and he did have an immense fortune with which to attract a wife.

"Perhaps you should consider returning to London," he suggested.

Winifred would have liked nothing better, but she could scarce admit to that to Nick. He needed her here to look out for him. "I am content to remain at Whitethorn Manor. Indeed, there are several matters here which require my personal supervision." She hoped he would not ask her to be more specific.

"Well, then," Nick said, looking thoughtful, "I will entrust the place to your keeping."

Too late, Winifred saw the trap. "Where will you be?"

"Maidstone. I plan to leave tomorrow and will remain there until after the summer Assizes."

"Business?"

He nodded. "A civil suit."

That sounded harmless enough, but Winifred was suspicious by nature. Her son was keeping something from her.

She would not rest until she discovered what it was.

5

Constance Crane tried in vain to blot out the insistent voice and ignore the damning questions it asked. This was not the first interrogation she had endured during the five weeks of her imprisonment.

"What person can unwitch what another doth bewitch?"

The answer was "a witch," but if she gave it, she would lay herself open to other questions, probing questions designed to trap her into saying more than she meant. She would be asked if the innocent herbal remedies her cousin concocted in her stillroom were charms for unwitching. Agree and they would say Lucy was a witch. Deny the charge and they would not believe her.

Constance's surroundings provided little to distract her. The room was empty save for the table behind which her inquisitors sat, forcing her to stand before them. The bare walls were broken by one small window. She knew it overlooked the marketplace, but she was not close enough to see out. Instead, she could stare only as far as the flies buzzing in the opening.

The small chamber smelled of frankincense, burned to counteract foul smells. Unable to wash for many days, her hem stained from the filth of her dank and noisome cell, Constance dared not imagine how rank an odor must emanate from her person. She could no longer smell herself but it was humiliating to think that others did. She had always prided herself on cleanliness, using her own preparation of orange-flower water as a scent.

"What person can unwitch what another doth bewitch?"

The coldness of Doctor Cole's voice sent a shiver through Constance's thin frame. She knew who—and what—he was. The guards who brought food to prisoners in Maidstone's gaol had been more than willing to provide details.

The Reverend Thomas Cole was now archdeacon of Essex, but years ago, when King Edward reigned, he'd been master of Maidstone's school. Later, during Queen Mary's restoration of the Church of Rome, he'd been obliged to go into exile, living first in Frankfort, then in Geneva. He'd returned to England when Queen Elizabeth took the throne and last year had played a prominent role in the trial of several witches from Chelmsford.

He believed in the effectiveness of both bewitching and unwitching.

So did most people, including Constance, although she was not so sure as Cole was that every cunning woman skilled with herbs was also a witch. The only thing of which she was certain was that she could not answer his question without creating more difficulties for herself.

"What person can unwitch what another doth bewitch?" he asked again.

Constance had lost track of how often she'd heard that particular demand for information, and she could no longer remember how many times she had been interrogated since her arrest. In the guise of a search for the truth, she had been subjected to endless badgering and bullying. A justice of the peace had ques-

tioned her the first time. Then she'd been turned over
to the tender mercies of the clergy.

"Do you dispute the power of witchcraft?" Cole's
companion, Adrian Ridley, spoke for the first time.

Unable to discern either sympathy or compassion in
Ridley's cold green eyes, Constance could only assume
he believed the lies, accepted that she was capable of
causing another's death. His indifference to her plight
was hurtful. In the months before her arrest, she had
begun to think of him as a friend, but it was clear he
did not intend to lift a finger to help her fight the
false charges laid against her. Neither, it seemed, would
anyone else. She and Lucy appeared to have been
abandoned by everyone. No family member, no friend,
not even a former foe, had come forward to offer help.

As she had from the start of the questioning, Constance held herself very still, watching and waiting. She
had learned to be self-effacing and patient during the
many long years she had served as a waiting gentlewoman to the marchioness of Northampton. She had
also gained an understanding of the way words could
be used as a trap. Since she could rely on naught but
her own wits to save her, she had no intention of being
tricked into condemning herself.

"The Scriptures say one must not suffer a witch to
live," Cole stated.

Constance managed not to shudder and made no
reply, but this time she felt the chill of fear clear to
the bone. To dispute the power of witchcraft was to
repudiate scriptural teaching on the matter. Doing so
could lead to being charged with heresy, and while
those convicted of witchcraft in England were sentenced to be hanged, those found guilty of heresy
might be burnt.

"Who was he, this Peter Marsh that died of witchcraft?" The sharpness of the query betrayed Cole's irritation over her failure to answer previous questions.

Again Constance maintained a stubborn silence. If she made any answer, she would be agreeing that Marsh had been bewitched to death. They would then accuse her of bewitching him and of failing to get another witch to unwitch him. If she denied these charges, they would insist he had been bewitched and charge her with failing to unwitch him after some other witch had cast a spell on him.

Ridley spoke in a soft voice, answering for her. "Marsh was clerk to Hugo Garrard before I entered his service as chaplain and took over both clerking and secretarial duties."

"What was he to her?" Cole demanded.

"They were . . . friends."

"Friends? Or lovers?"

Anger at last spurred Constance into speech. "We were never lovers."

"He desired you." Ridley's green eyes shot sparks. "Did he force himself upon you, mistress? Did you revenge yourself upon him for ill-using you?"

"Peter Marsh never gave me cause to want him dead."

They did not listen. They had already decided she had bewitched a man to death. They merely wanted her to confess.

Constance glared at Ridley, hating herself for having once found him attractive. The plain black gown of a clergyman did not hide the fact that he was a well-formed man with chiseled features and thick, ebony-hued hair. When they'd first met, Constance had thought him charming, but he exuded no charm whatsoever when he resumed his questioning.

"You and Mistress Milborne were seen kneeling in a garden. How many times have you lain flat or knelt in that place?" Other clergymen had already tried to get her to admit to this. Constance did not answer Ridley, either.

Exhaustion, she thought, had weakened her resolve. She had been foolish to let him lure her into saying as much as she had.

She longed to lie flat right here on the stone-flagged floor. She could not remember the last time she'd slept well. Rest did not come easy when one shared accommodations with rats and other vermin.

"In the yard or house, kneeling, standing, or lying flat, did you ever speak these words: 'Christ, my Christ, if thou be a Savior, come down and avenge me of mine enemies, or else thou shalt not be a Savior.' "

The prayer was that of a committed apostate. It implied that if Christ did not help the supplicant, she would turn instead to the devil. Constance wanted to deny she'd ever uttered such heretical sentiments, but it seemed wisest to maintain her silence. She stiffened her spine and said nothing.

"Will you confess you killed a lamb by witchery?" Cole posed this question.

Constance was unable to stifle a sigh. Had she known the trouble one lamb could cause, she'd have minded her own business. "I have explained the matter of the lamb," she said in a weary voice.

For just a moment she thought she saw a flicker of pity in Ridley's eyes, but it vanished as quickly as it had come.

"Explain again," Cole ordered.

Since she could see no way they could use the incident against her, Constance complied. "In the spring, I came upon one of my neighbors feeding a lamb with milk and white bread. I remarked that this was wasteful, since it took bread and milk from the mouths of children."

"But the lamb died."

"Aye, it did. Most like from surfeit of milk and bread."

"Do you say this was God's will?"

Pressing her hands to her temples, Constance tried to think. Was this another trick? If she agreed the lamb's death was God's will, would they accuse her of praying to God to kill it?

"The lamb died because it was passing weak when it was born. Not even good bread and milk could save it."

Cole turned to Adrian Ridley. "The lamb's sickness and death and the death of Peter Marsh were caused by the devil operating through this witch."

Constance felt the color drain from her face. A wave of dizziness hit her at the same time, making her sway. What was the use? They would twist whatever she said and misinterpret what she did not to suit themselves. That there was a simple reason for the lamb's death meant nothing because there was no rational explanation for what had happened to Peter Marsh. One day he had been fit as a prize bull. The next he had been dead.

6

Three blue-eyed, small-boned sprites sat on cushions in a circle on the floor of Lady Appleton's study. They followed the same routine every day, joining one dark-haired, dark-eyed imp as playmates and companions after they broke their fast. At lessons, which began at midmorning, Lady Appleton strove to treat them with equal fairness, but Rosamond, her late husband's bastard, held a special place in her heart, in spite of the circumstances of her birth.

The oldest scholar was Lady Appleton's goddaughter and had been named for her. She was not yet seven years old.

"Have you the answer, Susan?" Lady Appleton asked, using the ekename the younger Susanna preferred.

Susan's mother, Jennet Jaffrey, hearing the question as she passed by the open door, paused to listen for the answer. Some had criticized Leigh Abbey's housekeeper for eavesdropping on other people's conversations, but Jennet justified her habit by arguing that it was helpful for those in charge to know what went on behind their backs. Besides, she could see no wrong in observing the children's lessons when three of the four youngsters were her own offspring.

Jennet peered around the jamb. Susan was chewing

on her lower lip in concentration, a habit she'd copied
from her mother, as she stared at the numbers she'd
inscribed on a pair of tables. Those wax tablets, bound
in pairs to protect their faces, were one of the child's
most treasured possessions.

Just as Susan was about to reply, Rosamond thrust
her slate under Lady Appleton's nose in a demand for
attention. She was too young yet to handle the stylus
used for writing on wax, let alone write on paper or
wield a knife to sharpen a quill.

Jennet's son, the youngest of her brood, imitated
Rosamond's action, though he had written nothing at
all on his slate. Two months older than Rosamond, he
was the little girl's shadow.

Jennet pursed her lips, struggling to conquer her ill
will toward the child, no easy task when Rosamond
resembled her deceased father more each day. She had
his looks—the narrow face and high forehead, the
dark brown, wavy hair, the deep brown eyes—though
in Rosamond they combined to make her a pretty
child. She also had Sir Robert Appleton's arrogance.
And his temper.

The little mistress, as the servants were wont to call
her, had been taken in at Leigh Abbey by her father's
widow when she was two. After another two years with
Lady Appleton, she scarce remembered her real
mother. It was Susanna Appleton she called Mama.

To her credit, Lady Appleton tried not to spoil the
child. She dressed her simply, in much the same sort
of clothing worn by Jennet's two daughters.

What worried Jennet was the way her son deferred
to Rosamond in everything, even accepting a new
name from her. She'd dubbed him Sir Mole during
one of their games, for the pale, mole brown color of
his hair, and now he would answer to nothing else.

Jennet had considered asking Lady Appleton to intervene and insist he be called Rob, but no one liked to remind the mistress that the boy had been her late husband's godson and namesake. Mole had stuck.

Lady Appleton praised Susan's work and checked Rosamond's sums and set Rob back to work on his ciphering. Rosamond snickered. In response, the boy gazed at her with a pup's adoration. He did not seem to care that she was better than he was at arithmetic.

Jennet sighed, impatient for the day when her son would turn six and could be put in breeches and sent to the village school. He'd learn far more with other lads.

"Ka-a-a-te!"

Susan's wail of protest jerked Jennet's attention away from her son. She was in time to see one daughter drop her stylus and attempt to box the other's oversized ears.

Like the mole-colored hair, those ears were the children's common legacy from their father. In every other way, five-and-a-half-year-old Kate differed from her siblings. She was outgoing where they were quiet. Unable to sit still for more than a quarter of an hour. Now she danced out of Susan's reach, into the sunbeams streaming in through the east-facing window, laughing in delight. Lady Appleton's soft-spoken words of reproof made no dent in her mischievous grin.

It grew broader still when the infection spread to the other children. Rob tried manfully to suppress his giggles, but Rosamond did not even make the attempt.

"Enough," Lady Appleton declared when all four children dissolved into laughter. "Go your ways. There will be no more lessons today."

But she called Rosamond back as the others left the room. Jennet remained where she was, just on the far side of the open door. She had a clear view of the two people standing in front of the huge *mappa mundi* hung on one paneled wall.

"I did not do it, Mama," Rosamond said.

Lady Appleton lifted one brow but let the child's comment pass unremarked.

Rosamond had always done something, Jennet thought, but it was second nature to her to deny any accusation.

She was her father's child.

"I am going away for a little while, Rosamond," Lady Appleton said. "I want you to promise me you'll be a good girl while I'm gone."

Unaware that any trip had been planned, Jennet moved into the study, coming to a halt just inside the heavy oak door. She kept one hand on the huge ring of keys suspended from her waist. They were the symbol of her position in the household and opened everything from the spice chest to Lady Appleton's stillroom, but they had an annoying tendency to jangle at inopportune moments.

"I will go with you," Rosamond declared.

"Not this time."

"Why not?"

Lady Appleton hesitated. "There is no need to disrupt your routine, Rosamond. I will be gone less than a fortnight."

"But I want to go with you." Rosamond's lower lip slid forward into a pout and she crossed her arms across her chest.

Foot stamping would come next. If Jennet had been able to place a wager on this, she'd have won. Lady Appleton tried to reason with the child first, a futile effort. Their discussion ended with Rosamond in tears and Lady Appleton obliged to play the heavy-handed parent. She sent for the nursery maid to carry Mistress

Rosamond, kicking and screaming, to confinement in her bedchamber.

Only after the child's outraged cries faded into the distance, did Jennet speak. "It appears, madam, that she does not want you to go."

As Lady Appleton had long since accepted that Jennet overheard things—in truth, that ability had proven most useful to her in the past—she did not comment on her housekeeper's knowledge of what had just transpired. Instead she asked, "Do you suppose she thinks I mean to desert her?"

"You have left Leigh Abbey ere now and always returned."

"Only a handful of times since she came to live with me and only twice have I left her behind." She sat at her writing table to sort through the papers piled there.

Jennet picked up several abandoned slates and stacked them atop a table already heavy-laden with leather-bound volumes. "You are not Lady Pendennis."

There was no reason to mince words. Rosamond's real mother had left the little girl to be fostered at Leigh Abbey in order to travel abroad with her new husband. They'd gone first to Poland, to the court of Sigismund Augustus, as representatives of Queen Elizabeth. Now they were in Sweden and showed no inclination to return to England.

"No, I am not Eleanor," Lady Appleton agreed. "But does Rosamond understand that?"

"Where are you going that you cannot take her with you?" Jennet asked.

"To Maidstone."

"For the Assizes?" Jennet brightened, remembering something a passing chapman had told her.

"I wish to spend some time in Nick Baldwin's company before he leaves England for an extended stay abroad." Lady Appleton's words were blunt, her meaning clear. "He has gone to stay in his town house in Maidstone." She rearranged the contents of her penner, straightening a goose-quill pen already shaved of feathers.

Shaken by the notion that her mistress would openly consort with a man, and a mere merchant at that, Jennet found herself at an uncharacteristic loss for words.

"I would like you to accompany me there, Jennet." Lady Appleton closed the fancy leather case with a snap. "We will endeavor to give every appearance of propriety while we are together in Maidstone."

"Are you sure that is possible, madam? I have heard that Maidstone is a most self-righteous place. In the spring, the corporation ordered the maypole removed, and 'tis said they frown on dicing and card playing in the taverns."

With any other employer, even an upper-level servant who so far forgot her place would have been sent packing, but Jennet had been with Lady Appleton for far too long to fear reprisals.

"We have no plans to play cards."

"Madam, think of your reputation. Your good name."

"How times have changed." There was more amusement than annoyance in Lady Appleton's voice. "Before you married Mark, I had similar fears for your virtue."

"I wed Mark before I let him bed me."

With startling abruptness, Lady Appleton's face lost its smile. She rose from her chair in a rush, towering over Jennet, who was only of middling height for a woman. Tight-lipped, she began to pace, passing the cold hearth with its marble chimneypiece, pausing before the small, carpet-draped table that held Venetian glass goblets and a crystal flagon of Rhenish wine, but then moving on, empty-handed, to the window seat. There she seized up a cushion and hugged it to her chest while she stood with her back to Jennet and stared out at the fields and orchards.

"Nick asked me to marry him. I said no."

"But if you—"

"You know my feelings on marriage, at least for myself."

"Better to marry than to become a mistress. What if you—"

Jennet broke off when Lady Appleton tossed aside the cushion and whirled about to face her. Eyes snapping in vexation, she was a daunting sight.

"Leave sermons to the vicar, Jennet. I mean to go to Maidstone and stay in Nick's house. The only matter open to question is whether you will accompany me."

Unable to hide how troubled she was by their exchange, Jennet's answer came out sounding stiff with disapproval. "I am yours to command, madam."

Lady Appleton hesitated. For just a moment, she seemed to waver. Then she straightened her shoulders and dismissed Jennet with a curt nod. "Good. See to the packing, then. We leave on Monday."

7

In the fashion made popular by the queens of France and England, Susanna rode her own horse using a sidesaddle. Her mare was sweet-tempered. The weather was perfect for travel. She could wish for nothing else to make the day perfect . . . except Jennet's approval.

Susanna regretted her sharp words to her housekeeper and the strained relations between them since that day. From the time Jennet had become Susanna's tiring maid, when Susanna was nineteen and Jennet only a bit more than three years younger, a bond had existed between the two women. By the time Jennet married Mark Jaffrey and assumed the post of housekeeper, she had also become Susanna's close companion and confidante.

Jennet would come around, Susanna assured herself. Indeed, the fact that she was just behind, perched on a pillion attached to the back of Lionel's saddle, seemed a favorable sign. Jennet could easily have made an excuse to remain at Leigh Abbey—her duties as housekeeper, the children, the fact that she abhorred riding. Susanna always felt a little guilty that she took so much pleasure in travel when it was abundantly clear that Jennet did not enjoy anything about it.

In spite of Jennet's air of martyrdom, Susanna reveled in the journey to Maidstone. They entered the town near dusk and rode down the High Street in the direction of the river crossing. Following Nick's directions, they turned south just before they reached the stone bridge, passing by the archbishop of Canterbury's palace and the parish church of All Saints. Both buildings showed their most opulent faces to traffic on the Medway, in effect turning their backs on the town.

Nick's house lay just beyond the church in part of what had once been a college of secular canons. At the dissolution of the monasteries, the buildings had passed into private hands. The resultant dwelling was small but pleasant and had the advantage of possessing its own stable and a minuscule garden.

To Susanna's disappointment, Nick was out when they arrived, but his man Simon was waiting for them and eager to show Susanna to the elegantly appointed room that would be hers for her visit. The garden lay just beneath her window. She could not see much of it in the rapidly falling darkness, but when she inhaled deeply she drew in the scents of roses, at least two separate varieties, and catmint, and honeysuckle, though it was late in the year for that.

She turned at the sound of someone entering the room behind her and smiled when she saw it was Nick. Before he could do more than grin back at her, Jennet came bustling in, a bounce in her step and a determined look on her face. She was followed by Susanna's henchmen, Lionel and Fulke, and two of Nick's servants, bringing with them a modest repast of cold meats and fruit for their supper. Nick's servants left once the meal had been set out.

Susanna's did not.

Resigned to their company for at least a little longer, Susanna dipped her hands into the bowl of scented water Jennet thrust toward her and washed her hands.

"We can serve ourselves," Nick told Lionel, who was second gardener at Leigh Abbey but often took on additional duties when his mistress traveled.

Even as a boy, he'd towered over Jennet. Now that he'd grown into his body, he was a formidable figure, lean and well muscled, with an air of confidence unusual in a servant. He was also, Susanna realized with a sense of surprise, quite a handsome young man, with sparkling hazel eyes and a cleft in his chin. He'd be breaking hearts all over Maidstone if they remained here long.

"Are you certain you need nothing more, madam?" Jennet asked.

An awkward silence fell. Fulke, Susanna's second manservant, a strapping, ruddy, rough-skinned fellow some two years Lionel's senior, grew even more red-cheeked than usual and avoided meeting her eyes.

Susanna cleared her throat. "We have had a long and tiring journey. I give you all leave to seek your beds. You, too, Jennet."

If all went well, Nick would provide the services usually performed by a tiring maid.

He opened the door and stood by it, waiting for the three of them to go.

A worried look on her face, Jennet followed Fulke and Lionel out. Then Nick dropped the bar into place to keep intruders out and Susanna forgot all about Jennet and Fulke and Lionel. For the rest of the night, every thought centered on her lover.

She woke later than was her custom the next day, though it was still early morning. For a moment she lay abed, uncertain where she was. She'd been pulled from sleep not by third cockcrow, which customarily came at dawn, but by the ringing of bells to mark the hour. Outside Nick's house she could hear sounds of traffic on both street and river— carts passing and boats, as well. Someone called a cheerful greeting to a friend. Another cursed a wagon moving slowly enough to block the road.

Maidstone.

No doubt the market began to sell fresh produce from the countryside at dawn, which was reckoned at five-of-the-clock at this time of year. The sun appeared even earlier than that.

"Awake?" a sleepy voice asked.

She rolled toward Nick's solid presence beside her in the bed, filled with a sense of contentment. Some time passed before they rose to share the simple tasks of washing faces and hands and dressing. This must be what it was like to be a new bride, she thought, bemused, if a woman married someone who cared for her.

"Jennet despairs of me," Susanna remarked a bit later.

Nick poured ale and sliced manchet bread to break their fast, then planted a kiss on her brow, one on her chin, and finally a third on her lips before he placed the simple meal in front of her.

For just a moment longer, she allowed herself to bask in the admiration reflected in his eyes, to revel in the afterglow of physical release, but in her heart she knew she must not give him false hope.

"I will miss you, Nick," she whispered, surprised by the catch in her voice.

He seated himself opposite her at the small, portable table set up to hold their food. "There's no necessity. I have asked you to come with me. Reconsider."

"I will not marry you, Nick."

"Well, then, give me one good reason why you cannot come visit me while I am in Hamburg."

"What excuse should I have to travel so far? I've no business there."

"You might wish to meet with German herbalists. Did you not tell me once that many fine herbals are written in German?"

"I read German, but I do not speak the language." That confession provoked an intrusive memory that had her avoiding Nick's too-perceptive gaze.

Robert had mocked her study of languages. Although, at times, they had been able to laugh together at her lamentable lack of ability to pronounce foreign words, at other times she had felt the sting of his criticism.

Nick was nothing like Robert, she reminded herself.

Except that they both wanted to make decisions for her.

"Look upon a journey to the Continent as an opportunity to expand your linguistic abilities." He paused to drain the last drops of ale from his mug. "Why, I can teach you the most common German phrases. And a sprinkling of Low Dutch, too." His eyes glinted wickedly, suggesting that the words he had in mind from that language were not the most respectable.

Susanna made another attempt to turn the conversation. "I also read Latin, Greek, French, and Spanish. Would you have me embark on voyages to those lands, as well?"

"The German states will suffice. And here is another enticement. Not only could you confer with the herbalists, you'd be able to talk to some of the most skilled mapmakers in all the world." Nick knew she was fascinated by maps that showed the topography of faraway places. "And you can talk to landowners," he added. "Learn new techniques of husbandry."

"Nick—"

" 'Tis the simplest thing in the world to take ship from London or any of the East Anglian ports." He reached for the pitcher of ale to refill his mug and missed Susanna's reaction. Of a sudden, she lost her appetite, remembering that there were other reasons why she could not do what Nick proposed.

Just the thought of being out on the open water in a ship again had her stomach twisting and her heart pounding fast. Vivid images flashed into her mind—a seagoing vessel foundering in a storm, a small rowing boat at the mercy of choppy waves. With an effort, Susanna forced the memories away and managed to breathe calmly and evenly. After a moment, her traitorous body returned to normal.

A glance at Nick told her he'd noticed nothing amiss. He was only now returning the majolica-ware pitcher to the sideboard.

He was still talking about ships. "Just a short passage across the North Sea and you will be—"

"Deathly ill," she cut in.

"Ill?" Momentary confusion abruptly turned to concern. "What is wrong, Susanna?"

Forcing a smile to assure him she had not contracted any disease apt to carry her off, Susanna resigned herself to explaining, at least in part. "You make me betray my deepest, darkest secret, Nick."

She'd tried to keep her tone of voice light but knew by the look on his face that she had not succeeded.

"Even the shortest journey over water makes me most violently sick to my stomach." That was as close as she could bring herself to describing the true nature of her affliction.

She hated this weakness in herself, especially when

she could not understand why it continued to grow worse with the passage of time. Common sense told her the reaction should become less intense, not more, and yet she could scarce argue with the evidence of her own senses. One fact was passing clear—she would not voluntarily venture out onto the choppy waters between England and the Continent.

Nick's brow had knit into a frown. "The shortest crossing can be made in a matter of hours in the right weather conditions."

"And if the winds be not favorable, even a fast ship can take weeks to reach shore again."

"There are remedies to still sickness caused by the sea."

Susanna again avoided his probing gaze. Certes, he must think it odd that she, an herbalist renowned for her knowledge, should not be able to cure such a mundane ailment.

He deemed her excuse petty. So it must seem, and the more so to one as widely traveled as Nick. Susanna despaired of making him understand her inexplicable fear of crossing over water when she did not fully comprehend it herself. In the end, she chose to let him believe she had a weak stomach, rather than admit to a weakness of spirit.

"For a short journey, I dose myself with ginger root, which allows me to manage a trip between London and Gravesend by tilt boat without disgracing myself." Or it had, until a little more than a year ago. "For a longer journey, that will not suffice."

She knew how to induce in herself a state in which she would feel nothing at all, not panic, not nausea, not even caution. But to continue thus for long would be dangerous. The same herbs that could bring calm and sleep could also deliver death.

Nick looked thoughtful. "Is that why you prefer

roads to waterways when you travel?" He did not wait for her reply. "What of river crossings?"

Susanna saw no censure in Nick's expression now. There was only concern, and a degree of understanding. She managed a faint smile. "Ferries make me queasy, but most times such a journey over water is so short that I can distract myself by watching those about me. Or the scenery."

She and Nick had never traveled together. Although he knew of some of the journeys she had made, he had never sat beside her in a wherry or stood with her, holding their horses' heads, as a barge was poled across a river.

"I could distract you." He rose and came around the table, slinging an arm around her shoulders and hauling her to her feet to be tucked in close against his side.

The gleam in his eyes sparked an answering response, astonishing Susanna. She'd thought she'd be sated by now.

But before Nick could do more than turn her in his arms to plant a gentle kiss on her lips, Jennet rushed into the room, skidding to a stop on the tiled floor at the sight of them. Susanna closed her eyes and slipped out of Nick's embrace. She heartily wished she'd had the foresight to restore the bar to the door after she'd returned from her visit to the privy.

"This had better be important," Nick muttered.

"What is it, Jennet?"

Jennet danced from foot to foot in excitement. "Two of the accused witches, madam. They are gentlewomen!"

Witches again! Susanna bit back a groan. Some two years back, Jennet had become convinced that a witch had put a curse on her. And then, in April, she had purchased a pamphlet from a chapman, an account of the previous year's trial of three witches in the neighboring county of Essex. Ever since, Jennet had displayed what seemed to Susanna to be an unhealthy fascination with the subject.

"What witches?" Nick asked.

"The witches in Maidstone gaol. They are to be tried at the Assizes. And two of them are most unusual. So say folk in the marketplace. All those who have been tried for witchcraft ere now were common folk."

The poor and the friendless, Susanna thought. Those with none to speak for them. "And these women?"

"They are kin to the lord of Mill Hall, near Hythe. Mistress Lucy Milborne and Mistress Constance Crane."

The second name provoked a sharp, unpleasant memory. "Is it possible?" she murmured.

"Are you acquainted with them?" Nick's quiet voice and the feel of his hand on her elbow steadied Susanna.

"I may know the second. There was a Constance Crane who served as a waiting gentlewoman to the late marchioness of Northampton."

Jennet's sharp intake of breath caught Nick's attention and had him narrowing his eyes. "This Constance—is she a friend?"

"Scarce that." The one time Susanna had talked to her, they'd parted on an acrimonious note. "She was one of Robert's mistresses."

Nick's expression turned thunderous. He had never cared for Susanna's husband alive and thought even less of Sir Robert Appleton since the revelation of certain dishonorable acts he had committed just before his death. "You've no obligation to her."

At his tone of voice, Susanna's brows lifted. She balked at being told what was best to do, as if she were a child incapable of making decisions for herself. One of Nick's most endearing qualities had always been his tolerance of her independent ways.

"You have gained no new rights where I am concerned," she said in a quiet but implacable voice. "If I wish to inquire further into this matter, I shall do so."

"Whether this is the same woman or not, you'd be wise to have naught to do with her."

"A gentlewoman has been accused of a terrible crime for which she may be executed if she is found guilty. It was not so long ago that I was in a similar situation. I can still remember how helpless I felt, locked away in a cell, accused of a crime I did not commit. I would not wish that fate on my worst enemy."

Constance, if it was she, was scarce that. Indeed, Susanna had felt a deep sympathy for the other woman once they'd met and talked. Constance had truly loved Robert. She'd hoped to marry him . . . before he'd wed Susanna.

"I cannot approve of this."

"I do not need your approval, Nick. This is a matter of simple justice." And, no doubt, a case of murder.

Susanna assumed that someone had died. The authorities would not have troubled themselves to make an arrest for less. But had the death been caused by sorcery? That she questioned. In her study of herbs, she had learned that most effects had a natural rather than a supernatural cause.

It did no good to try and convert others to her peculiar way of thinking. Superstitions were too deeply ingrained in most people to be rooted out by mere logic. Generation after generation had frightened themselves and their offspring with tales of evil forces abroad in the night. Susanna had long since realized she had no hope of dispelling Jennet's belief in witchcraft. Even Nick, for all his practical nature, was convinced such beings existed and could do harm.

Resigned, she turned to Jennet. "Where is the gaol?"

"You cannot mean to go there, madam."

"Mistress Crane is accused of witchcraft, Susanna." By his tone of voice, Nick's disapproval had not decreased, but now it did seem to be overshadowed by concern for her safety.

"Madam, you must not involve yourself!" Jennet's impassioned protest startled Susanna. "Think, madam, of the danger! If you attempt to help someone accused of witchcraft, you may be suspected of being a witch yourself."

"Nonsense."

"Is it worth the risk?" Nick asked. "Given your well-known expertise with herbs, the business has vast potential for disaster. Ignorant men might leap to all manner of dangerous conclusions."

Susanna could not deny the wisdom of their admonitions. Still, she could not in good conscience let Constance, or any other gentlewoman, be tried on such a charge without at least inquiring into the circumstances.

"I only mean to visit the gaol. What harm in that?"

"What do you think you can accomplish?" Nick sounded disgruntled. "Maidstone Assizes convene ten days hence. That is not enough time to do more than commiserate with the accused."

Little time indeed, Susanna thought, but if she did nothing, then less than a fortnight from now Constance would be beyond human help. The judges sat but two days. Convicted felons were customarily hanged the day after court adjourned.

Susanna went up to Nick and brushed her lips against his cheek. "Do not worry before there is need. For the nonce I am naught but a charitable gentlewoman taking alms to poor prisoners."

8

Faith," Jennet whispered as she stepped from bright daylight into the darkness of the gaol cell.

Just ahead of her, Lady Appleton lifted a lantern and called out Constance's name. The candle behind the thick horn panes did little to illuminate the small room. Although the gaol was located in the center row of the High Street, between the corn cross and the butter market, the noise and bustle outside barely penetrated its thick stone walls.

It was too much to hope, Jennet supposed, that this would turn out to be a different Constance Crane. And that meant it was all her fault that Lady Appleton intended to involve herself in the case. She'd been too hasty, Jennet admitted. Too anxious to interfere. She'd seized on the first excuse to interrupt her mistress and Master Baldwin. Far better to have let them continue what they were doing!

When her eyes began to adjust, Jennet was able to locate the prisoners, two women attached by shackles to the inner wall. The wavering beam of light fell first on the one sitting on the dirt floor in the near corner. Her arms were wrapped tight around her upraised knees and her head rested upon them. Her coif was askew, revealing scraggly strands of thinning, yellow-white hair that suggested she was much too old to have been Sir Robert's mistress.

When she lifted her head, Jennet bit back a gasp. The woman was trough-eyed, her left eye much lower than the right. No wonder she had been accused of witchcraft! Never had Jennet seen such an evil countenance.

Heart racing, Jennet shifted her gaze to the second prisoner, who was struggling to stand despite the iron chains that held her. This one was younger than her companion but a far cry from what Jennet had come to expect in one of Sir Robert's mistresses. She was at least as old as Lady Appleton, perhaps older. Furthermore, she must have been exceeding thin even before she was put in gaol.

Once on her feet, the woman swayed. Lady Appleton stepped forward to offer assistance but was stopped by a glare that left no doubt in Jennet's mind that help was unwelcome.

Good. She could not be the same Constance Crane. And she wanted them gone. Jennet was ready to leave.

Lady Appleton lingered.

As they watched, the prisoner braced her back against the stone wall, squared her thin shoulders, and looked full at them both. Even in the dimness, Jennet could see recognition dawn on the woman's face. She went still as death, her features frozen.

The corner of one eye appeared to have a distinct droop.

If Jennet had harbored any remaining doubt, the expression on Lady Appleton's face was enough to tell her that, against all odds, this was the same Constance Crane

"Come to gloat?" Sir Robert's former mistress spoke in a raspy voice caused, Jennet suspected, by the dampness in the cell.

"I am here to help, if I can. Are you innocent of the crime of which you stand accused?"

"I am accused of murder by witchcraft and my cousin here is said to have killed another man by putting a curse on him. As the old rhyme goes, 'If I be a witch, the devil thee twitch.' "

Holding her breath, her hands clasped tightly together, Jennet waited for the quivering and quaking to begin.

Nothing happened.

Lady Appleton did not seem surprised. She met Mistress Crane's obvious contempt with a bracing tone of voice. "These charges are untrue. Why were they made against you?"

"You believe me?" Her face betraying both confusion and relief, Mistress Crane slumped against the wall. Her brief spurt of defiance seemed to have used up all her strength.

Filled with reluctant sympathy for the prisoner, Jennet wondered how long she had been held in gaol and what means had been used to examine her.

"I do not know why," Mistress Crane insisted. "I do not understand any of what has happened to us."

Tears sprang into her eyes and she dashed them away with impatient fists. She must be embarrassed to be seen like this by her old lover's widow, Jennet thought. Unless she was past caring what anyone thought of her plight.

Jennet kept her distance but Lady Appleton once more attempted to approach. Mistress Crane's reaction was immediate. Fending off any offer of comfort with a ferocious scowl, she flattened herself against the wall. Lady Appleton retreated, but not before Jennet was able to compare the two of them. For just a moment, they'd stood side by side, illuminated by the lantern.

Both had brown hair and blue eyes, but there the physical similarities seemed to end.

Mistress Crane was several inches shorter and by far the thinner of the two. She had a sharp beak of a nose and a small, pointed chin. Lady Appleton's features were more substantial, to go with a square jaw some said was the outward sign of her determined nature.

"You must not give up hope, Constance. If you say there was no witchcraft involved, then I believe you and I will do all I can to help you prove it. The first thing we must do is find another way to account for the deaths. If we can prove someone else murdered those people and explain why, the authorities must perforce set you free."

"Why do you care? You have no reason to help me and every excuse to continue to leave me here to rot." Her eyes narrowed. "What do you gain by appearing here now?"

"Justice."

The simplicity of Lady Appleton's explanation seemed to startle Mistress Crane. She started to speak, then thought better of it. She waited for Lady Appleton to take the lead.

"To begin with, you must tell me all you know of these two deaths, starting with the names of the victims and how they were connected with you."

Jennet searched the cramped cell, hoping to spot a chair or a stool. Her mistress would be more comfortable seated. The conditions in the gaol would make her leg throb if they stayed much longer. Ever since she'd injured it in a fall some years earlier, excessive damp troubled her.

A straw pallet was the only furniture. It moved suspiciously when Jennet poked at it with her toe. Withdrawing her foot a safe distance, she decided that if the two women shared their quarters with a rat, she did not need proof of it.

"My cousin is accused of killing Clement Edgecumbe," Mistress Crane said.

"Who was he and how did he die?"

"He was her neighbor. He fell into a trance from which none could wake him and, after eight hours, died."

Jennet felt her face pale. She was no expert on herbs but she'd learned enough from Lady Appleton over the years to know that if Master Edgecumbe had not been bewitched to death, he might have been poisoned.

"Was Mistress Milborne near Clement Edgecumbe before this happened?" Lady Appleton asked.

"No. Nor did she send him any gifts of food or drink. But they'd quarreled the previous Sunday, over some trivial point in the vicar's sermon."

"Was any accusation made at the time?"

Mistress Crane shook her head. "Lucy was charged when I was. Neither of us had any warning that something was amiss until we were arrested."

"Anyone suspecting another of witchcraft must lay information against that person with the constable or local justice," Lady Appleton mused aloud. "Who gave information in Lucy's case?"

The old woman spoke for the first time. "Mildred Edgecumbe, widow of Clement. That spiteful cow! If I'd been inclined to hex someone, 'twould have been her."

She subsided again after this outburst, once more lowering her head onto her knees. Jennet, watching her closely, thought she saw her make the Papist sign of the cross.

"What of the man you are accused of killing?" Lady Appleton asked Mistress Crane.

"His name was Peter Marsh."

"Was he known to you?"

A cackle erupted from the older woman, though she did not trouble to look at them. Mistress Crane's face blossomed with bright color.

"Ah," Lady Appleton said.

"No! That is only what they say of me." Mistress Crane spoke in a choked voice, as if she struggled to hold back tears. "Peter and I were friends but I never gave myself to him. And he never gave me cause to want him dead."

Skeptical, Jennet felt little sympathy, but Lady Appleton patted Mistress Crane's arm and murmured soothing words. "Did no one speak in your defense?"

Again, confusion showed on Mistress Crane's face. She shook her head, as if to clear her mind, before she answered.

"We have another cousin, Hugo Garrard. He is head of the family and resides at Mill Hall, where I have been housekeeper since Lady Northampton died."

Bitterness twisted her features.

"I thought he meant to help us, but we have been here for weeks, Lady Appleton, and he has done perilous little on our behalf. We have been insulted time and again in the guise of being questioned, and again and again we have been accused of things neither of us has done. I was acquainted with Peter Marsh. That much is true. And he was a handsome man. But I never allowed him to ill-use me, as the clergymen who interrogated me appear to mean the term. That being true, how could I become angry enough to kill him for refusing to marry me? The subject of marriage was never raised between us!"

Ill-used her, then refused to marry her. The charges had a familiar ring to them, but Jennet could not place where she might have heard them before. She stopped trying to remember when Lady Appleton asked Mistress Crane to recount all she could recall of the period just before Marsh's body was found.

The tale riveted Jennet's attention. Gathering plants under the full moon. A messenger sent at dawn from Mill Hall to Edgecumbe Manor. The body under the tree. And a wych elm, too!

Jennet shuddered in delight at this last detail. Let Lady Appleton say what she would, Jennet believed that witches had the power to hex and to kill. And if ever she had seen a woman who looked like a witch, it was Constance Crane's trough-eyed cousin.

9

By the time Constance had finished recounting the events leading up to her arrest, Susanna had come to a conclusion. The woman was guilty of nothing more criminal than befriending an older, infirm relative.

On the surface, there was little anyone could do to help her and yet Susanna felt impelled to try. Once she had been jealous of Constance, but that time was long past. Although Susanna could not explain the bond she'd come to feel with some of her husband's former mistresses, neither could she deny its existence. In part, it was guilt that urged her to offer Constance her assistance. The man who had deceived and disappointed Constance had been Susanna's husband. With his death, she had inherited all he'd had, including the responsibility, when she was able, to right old wrongs.

She leveled a direct look at Constance. "You say you have been questioned?"

"All too often."

"By whom?"

"Constable. Archdeacon. Justice of the peace. Clerk of the court. Clergyman." She ticked them off on dirty fingers with broken nails.

"Were you called before the church court?"

"No, but only because there has not been time. I have told every one of them the same thing. I am no witch. I did no one harm, nor even wished harm upon him."

With every word, Susanna felt more keenly a sense of outrage at the injustice of Constance's treatment. If she did not help Constance, no one would.

"What of Mistress Milborne?"

The older woman did not look up at her name. She sat slumped against the wall, her head bowed.

Constance hesitated, then said in a quiet, despairing voice, "Lucy refuses to recognize the authority of those who question her."

Remembering her own reading of the pamphlet Jennet had acquired from the chapman, as well as bits and pieces of gossip she'd heard about other witchcraft trials, Susanna phrased her next question with care. "Have Lucy's neighbors been in the habit of consulting her as they would a cunning woman?"

"She has a small herb garden," Constance admitted, "but where is the harm in that? So do most housewives."

"Indeed. A necessity if one wishes to keep the household healthy."

"Lucy was ill much of the winter. I nursed her. I would have known if she engaged in any evil practices and I swear to you that she did not."

Susanna was willing to accept Constance's word that she did not believe her cousin was a witch, but that did not answer her question. "Cunning men and women do no evil but they do cast spells and sell charms and even unwitch those who believe themselves bewitched."

Constance stole a look at her kinswoman and seemed startled when Lucy at last decided to speak.

" 'Tis my calling they hold against me," she mumbled.

"Calling?" Puzzled, Susanna waited for her to elaborate, wondering if she was about to hear a confession of witchcraft, after all.

Before anyone could say more, the door to the cell opened to admit a tall man in the black robes of a clergyman. Ignoring Constance, Lucy, and Jennet, the newcomer turned suspicious green eyes on Susanna.

Startled by his sudden appearance and his rudeness, she stared back, assessing him in much the same way he examined her. His face seemed at odds with his clothing, having a male beauty no woman could miss noticing. Such handsome features, together with broad shoulders and coal-black hair, would have made him a welcome addition at the royal court, had he not had such a disapproving way about him.

"Lady Appleton of Leigh Abbey." His voice was mild but there was annoyance beneath the surface politeness.

"Do I know you, sir?"

"Only in passing."

"I would not have forgotten you."

"We never met face-to-face. I remained hidden in your stables, my features concealed, and departed the following day to take ship."

The extreme plainness of his garb had already indicated the likelihood he'd been in exile during the reign of Queen Mary, when a return to Catholicism had been forced on all good Englishmen, and those who refused to be converted, in particular those who had preached the New Religion from the pulpit, had fled the country to avoid being burnt to death as heretics. Susanna had helped many of them to escape.

How young and idealistic she had been then, she thought. She had even believed her marriage could be a happy one, that Robert would approve of the risks she took for her father's friends and for others who believed as they did.

How naive she had been! When Robert had discovered she'd made Leigh Abbey into a way station for those persecuted by Queen Mary, he'd been horrified. If it would not also have made his own position at court untenable, he'd have turned her over to the authorities. A few years later, however, when Queen Elizabeth restored the New Religion and banned Catholicism, Robert was quick to turn coat and claim credit for his wife's activities.

Struck by a thought, Susanna glanced at Lucy. An old woman, living in her own cottage, might well cling to the religion of her youth. Was that at the root of her trouble with her neighbors?

The clergyman spoke, drawing Susanna's attention back to him. "I am Adrian Ridley. From Leigh Abbey I journeyed to Strassbourg, but I spent the greater portion of my exile in Geneva."

That meant he now took the most extreme view of religion, that he opposed every trace of Papist tradition left in England's church, and that he'd be apt to find evil everywhere, even in places where it did not dwell.

"Sir Adrian is the chaplain at Mill Hall." From her tone, Constance begrudged him the title, though priests as well as knights were by custom accorded the same form of address.

"Hugo Garrard sent me to Maidstone to help his cousins."

"Liar!" Constance shrieked the word and flung herself toward him, stopped from assaulting him only by the chains that held her to the wall. "Your kind of help will send us straight to the gallows!"

He stepped toward her in spite of the risk of having his eyes scratched out and murmured something

Susanna could not catch. The tone, however, seemed soothing, which surprised her.

Constance spat in his face. "You asked who has questioned me, Lady Appleton. This man has."

"I do not want your death, Constance." Ridley wiped away the spittle but did not retreat. "Nor that of your cousin."

A disbelieving snort issued from Lucy's huddled figure.

"You want us to confess to things we have not done."

"Confess and be saved." Adrian Ridley was nose-to-nose with her now and all but shouting back.

Unnoticed by either of them, Susanna signaled to Jennet that it was time to depart. They would accomplish nothing further as long as Sir Adrian remained, and he gave no indication he meant to leave any time soon.

10

The solid thunk of the heavy door closing behind Susanna Appleton and her companion broke the spell of Adrian Ridley's angry green eyes. Constance blinked rapidly, feeling as if she'd just come out of a trance, then realized with a sinking heart what had happened.

"You drove them away!"

"I did nothing of the kind. Constance, you—"

"Get out! Stop badgering me!"

"Trust me to help you."

"Why should I? You have already betrayed what trust I once placed in you."

"If you will but humble yourself—"

"I will never say that I am a witch."

"Not even to save your life?"

"Hah!" She rattled her chains at him.

"To hear confession is forbidden," Lucy muttered.

They both turned to stare at her, but she was not looking at them. She kept her head down, clasped her knees, and rocked back and forth, back and forth, until Constance began to fear for her sanity.

"Will you not try to save your cousin?" Adrian asked. "Even if she is no witch, she is damned for her failure to give up the old ways."

"How can you expect her to? Would you give up your calling?"

"She must embrace the New Religion. And you must both tell the truth. Only then can you hope your lives will be spared."

"We have told the truth! You refuse to believe it." As tears threatened, she turned her head away from him, unwilling to let him see her weep. "Go away. Leave us in peace."

Instead, he addressed Lucy. "Repent, Mother Milborne. I can save you if you will but admit your heresy."

"Which heresy, preacher? Witchcraft, or being a good daughter of Rome?" Of a sudden she sounded almost cheerful.

In astonishment, Constance realized that Lucy took perverse delight in baiting the clergymen. It was a dangerous practice just now, but Constance did nothing to thwart her cousin's small pleasure.

Most likely nothing either of them did or said would make any difference in the end.

Lady Appleton had said she would do all she could to help prove their innocence, but Constance did not dare hope for much. If Robert's widow had truly meant to come to their aid, she would not have waited so long to act on the request in Constance's letter.

11

Nick Baldwin did not like what he learned during the time Susanna spent with the prisoners. When Susanna and Jennet returned to the house and he heard Constance Crane's story, he made one more attempt to convince them not to meddle.

"Jennet is right to be concerned," he told Susanna. "While you were at the gaol, I talked to Richard Emery. He is assistant to John Glascock, clerk of assizes for Kent. There are four women being held on charges of witchcraft, the other two in the common cell since they are not gently born. Emery tells me at least one of the clergymen involved in questioning Constance has been trying to establish some connection among them all."

"Is there a connection?"

"If there is, it has not yet been discovered. One woman is from Boughton Monchelsea, the other from Bethersden."

"Scarce neighbors of Mill Hall."

"Nor friends, and yet there is a common thread. The widow of Boughton Monchelsea is accused of bewitching to death a child by means of enchantment and potion. The charge against her claims she was incited by the instigation of the devil."

Susanna fixed on the word *potion,* as Nick expected she would. "She is a healer?"

"So it seems. At the least, she administered the wrong cure and her patient died."

"And the other woman?"

"She is also known to deal in herbal cures."

"As is Lucy Milborne."

"If the justices wish to pursue it, even 'intent to cure' is punishable under the current law against witchcraft."

"Punishable how?"

"By a year in prison."

He saw the consternation on her face, but beneath it was the stubbornness that both attracted him and made him fear for her safety. She accepted the risk that she might herself be accused of being a witch.

"Should a second person afterward be killed or destroyed by charm or witchcraft, or even by a cure improperly administered, the witch is tried as a felon."

"And hanged."

"And hanged," he agreed.

"I cannot let innocent women die." Susanna met his gaze, unflinching. "Nine full days remain before the Assizes begin. Time enough to journey to Mill Hall and discover for myself what transpired there."

Nick was uncertain such a venture would help Constance Crane or her cousin, but it would take Susanna way from Maidstone and those witch-hunting clergymen. As much as he'd wanted this time here with her, he suspected the shiretown was not the safest place for her just now. "Very well," he said. "I will go with you."

"No, Nick. I need you to stay in Maidstone. Arrange for food and drink and clean clothing to be sent to the prisoners. And bath water. All the female prisoners, not just Constance and Lucy Also, I wish to know more about this chaplain, Adrian Ridley, sent by Hugo Garrard to help his cousins. Constance feels he has done naught but assist the authorities against them. I would know why."

"You want me to strike up an acquaintance with this fellow?"

"Will you?" Her eagerness both charmed him and filled him with dismay.

Stepping close to her, he took her hands in his, dropping his voice too low for Jennet to hear his words. "I can deny you nothing, but I'd have been happier locking you in the bedchamber we shared last night and keeping you there until the Assizes are over.

12

WEDNESDAY, JULY 2, 1567

For Jennet the journey from Maidstone to Mill Hall was pure torture. She disliked travel on horseback in the best of conditions, and this route, though it followed the straight course of an old Roman road, was rough, hard, and narrow. Dust rose in huge, choking clouds with every step their mounts took.

"Better suited for sheep than people," Lionel agreed in a cheerful voice. He delighted in annoying her, and since she rode on a pillion attached to the back of his saddle, she was obliged to endure his close company for the entire trip. "Drovers from Romney Marsh bring their herds this way to market."

He and Fulke fell into a discussion of Welsh cattle. It seemed many people from the area of Mill Hall went to Maidstone to buy the beasts at the October fair, fattened them up on Romney Marsh, then drove them north again, all the way to London, to sell.

Lady Appleton rode ahead, taking obvious pleasure in their surroundings as they passed through the Weal-don Hills. From high, wooded ground, inhabited by deer and foxes and wild pigs, they descended to tree-lined lanes flanked by cultivated fields.

Only when they reached Aldington and were nearly

at their destination did Jennet take much interest in the landscape. Before that, she'd been too busy feeling sorry for herself. And worrying about what Lady Appleton had gotten them into this time. And fearing that they might make detours to Boughton Monchelsea and Bethersden en route.

At Aldington the archbishop of Canterbury's country palace rose on landlocked cliffs overlooking Romney Marsh and the port of Hythe. The manor could not fail to impress. In addition to a magnificent residence, it included nine enormous tithe barns, six stables, and eight dovehouses.

From Aldington the road ran parallel to the River Stour and was soon joined by Stone Street, another old Roman road. "The traveling will be easier the rest of the way," Lady Appleton said.

"Easier still did we turn east," Jennet muttered. According to the signpost, Canterbury was twelve miles distant. To reach Leigh Abbey they'd have to ride but another five.

As the long day drew to a close, they at last reached Mill Hall land. Where the fields they'd passed by earlier had been enclosed by shaws of oak, birch, or ash, Master Garrard used post and rail fences to keep his sheep from wandering. These impertinent beasts stared at Jennet through eyes set in wide heads with white faces and coal black noses.

Mill Hall had been built of warm red brick. The house stood at one side of the main group of fields, with kitchens, milk house, brew house, and bake house, all under the same roof as the living rooms. Hugo Garrard himself came out to meet them as the party clattered into his courtyard. Lady Appleton had sent word ahead to warn of her arrival.

Jennet saw at once that Master Garrard shared the family affliction. In his case it was only a slight droop in one eyelid, a defect scarce noticeable if one did not look for it. In part its presence was disguised by the heaviness of his eyelids.

A tall man, as thin as his cousin, Master Garrard looked no more than five and twenty, but he had old eyes, a faded blue in color. As he watched Lady Appleton dismount, he tugged with nervous fingers at his little tuft of a beard. It matched his reddish brown hair for color. The deep voice that bade them welcome invited them to stay the night but contained no hint of warmth.

"You are most gracious," Lady Appleton told him. "We will impose upon you no longer than we must, although I am certain you wish to do all you can to help free your cousins."

Hugo Garrard's smile looked forced as he played the gallant host, taking Lady Appleton's arm to escort her inside his house.

Ignoring her aching backside, Jennet hurried after them. She was in time to hear Master Garrard insist they postpone their proposed visit to Lucy Milborne's cottage until morning.

"It is not a good place to be with night coming on," he added.

Now that Jennet was off the back of that accursed horse, her energy returned and her natural curiosity revived with a vengeance. Master Garrard's comment intrigued her. Dusk was at least an hour away and if she'd understood Mistress Crane's account, Mistress Milborne lived near at hand.

Master Garrard, however, could not be persuaded. He ended the discussion by ordering a servant to show his gently born guest to her bedchamber.

"Does he believe his cousins guilty?" Jennet asked the moment she and Lady Appleton were left alone there.

"He may. Most people do believe in witches." She sent a wry smile in Jennet's direction. "I know full well that my views on the subject are shared by few others. Most people would consider them heretical."

Jennet paled. "Madam, it is not a matter for joking."

But instead of listening to Jennet's litany of concerns, Lady Appleton declared herself in need of a nap and suited action to words. Jennet was left with naught to do but unpack and clean her mistress's boots. Time dragged until they were summoned to supper.

When they arrived in the great hall, Master Garrard conducted Lady Appleton to the place of honor next to him at the high table. Jennet thought his hospitality now seemed a trifle less grudging, although he signaled for servants to bring water, basins, and towels for hand washing in the same peremptory manner he'd displayed earlier. Once these had been used and cleared away, he stood to recite the prayer before the meal. His chaplain, Jennet recalled, was still in Maidstone.

"All things depend upon thy providence, O Lord," he began, "to receive at thy hands due sustenance in time convenient. Thou givest to them and they gather it. Thou openest thy hand and they are satisfied with good things."

Assuming Master Garrard was done, since he fell silent, Jennet reached for the bread. Before she could lay a finger on it, the stream of words resumed. With each phrase he sounded more pompous.

When this soliloquy had continued for some minutes, Jennet began to wonder if the fellow might not be exaggerating his piety for effect. This pretentious prattling struck her as an effort to seem more religious than, in truth, he was.

"O heavenly Father," Master Garrard intoned,

"which art the fountain and full treasure of all goodness, we beseech thee to show thy mercies upon us thy children and sanctify these gifts which we receive of thy merciful liberality, granting us grace to use them soberly and purely, according to thy blessed will."

Again, Jennet's hand crept toward the bread. Again she had to pull back when the droning voice resumed the prayer.

"Hereby we acknowledge thee to be the author and giver of all good things and above all remember continually to seek the spiritual food of thy word, wherewith our souls may be nourished everlastingly, through our Savior Christ, who is the true bread of life, which came down from heaven, of whom whosoever eatest shall live forever and reign with Him in glory, world without end."

Jennet hesitated.

"So be it." He sat down, draped his napkin over his shoulder, and began to eat.

On the dais, there was little conversation. From her vantage point below, Jennet got the impression that Master Garrard gave only monosyllabic answers to Lady Appleton's remarks.

She had no better luck gleaning information from the upper servants seated at her table. Arthur Kennison, the man Mistress Crane had said carried messages between Mill Hall and Edgecumbe Manor, was already deep in his cups before the meal had scarce begun. The broken veins in his nose and the ruddy color of his cheeks suggested to Jennet that his state was not uncommon. It would have served her purpose well if he'd been the sort of drunkard to grow verbose and loquacious when he imbibed, but he was a silent, surly lout. He took no notice of her, and the rest of the company proved equally close-mouthed.

Even for a fish day, the food was uninspired. Jennet

consumed it in sullen silence, wondering why she had not elected to remain at Leigh Abbey when she'd had the chance.

The unending dullness of their stay at Mill Hall continued after supper. Someone played a lute, but with indifferent talent. The boy who tried to sing mangled every tune. Master Garrard did at last begin to talk to Lady Appleton, but only of crops and the weather and the pinnace he'd recently hired to carry fruit and vegetables from Hythe around the coast of Kent and up the Thames to London. She'd stop at Maidstone on her return voyage, he said, to add on a cargo of that bulky local commodity, fuller's earth.

"Cheaper to move freight by water," Master Garrard proclaimed. He became expansive on this dull subject, telling his captive audience 'twas a penny a mile by water when the cost ranged from fourpence to twelvepence a mile over land. Even sailing the long way around the coast, he insisted, produced a great savings.

Bored by such talk, Jennet was glad when she had an excuse to escape.

On her return from the privy at the far side of the kitchen yard she found herself moving more and more slowly, reluctant to go back inside. Just as she paused to look up at the stars, a man stepped out of the shadows, startling her by grabbing her arm and causing her to drop the candle she carried.

"Unhand me, sirrah!" Jennet opened her mouth to scream but closed it again when he made a shushing sound. More intrigued than frightened, she held her peace.

"Hear me out, I beg of you." He spoke in a whisper.

"Why should I?" Her heart beat at a furious rate. At last, something interesting was happening.

"Because you are curious?"

He had her there. "Well, fellow? What have you to say?"

She squinted, trying to discern his features. By the faint beams of the lantern hung by the door she could see that the stranger was tall, a head higher than most men she knew, and beanpole thin, even scrawnier than Master Garrard. By the feel of them, large, strong hands were appended to those stick-like arms.

"I know who your mistress is and why she came here and where she means to go on the morrow." For all the cockiness of this whispered speech, he stumbled a bit over the words.

Nervous? Fascinated out of any remaining apprehension, Jennet made no further attempt to free herself. "Everyone in this household knows as much by now."

"Warn her off. Do not let her go to the witch's cottage."

"Why should I take your advice? Who are you?"

He glanced from side to side, as if to make sure they were not observed. His grip tightened on her arm. "The cottage is located near the Street of Demons."

Jennet sucked in a breath. "How did it come by such a name?"

"How do you think? The entire area is a lonely and remote place well known to be the haunt of ghosts, smugglers, and witches."

"Who are you?" Jennet demanded again. "What do you know of witches?"

"I mean to know everything."

For some reason, that statement alarmed Jennet more than anything else her captor had said. She pulled, freeing herself from his grasp with surprising ease, and retreated a few steps. When there was a little distance between them, she spoke. "If Constance Crane was not afraid to visit her cousin, there can be no real danger."

"Constance Crane is also a witch." The words exploded in quick bursts. Then he muttered something else that Jennet could not catch.

"What did you say?"

"Evil haunts this region," the stranger repeated.

"Who are you?" she asked for the third time. The longer she was alone with him, the more he began to unnerve her, and yet she was resolved to learn more of his purpose.

"There are witches everywhere," he said.

"Why should I believe you when I do not know who you are?" Jennet was appalled to hear a quiver in her voice.

The man seemed to consider her question. The silence lengthened between them and she shivered, although the night was warm. The notion that this fellow might himself be a witch . . . or worse . . . made her heart speed up and her breath catch.

When a door opened nearby, they both jumped.

Hands pressed to her lips, Jennet spun toward the sound. It was Lionel, on his way to the privy. The knowledge that he would hear her if she cried out gave her renewed courage. She turned back to her companion, meaning to insist he answer. If he did not, she'd order Lady Appleton's henchman to apprehend him.

But there was no longer anyone behind her. The stranger had vanished into the blackness.

13

Maidstone had entirely too many inns. Nick had to visit five of them before he reached the east side of Gabriel Hill and discovered Adrian Ridley had a room at The Ship.

Striking up a conversation with a stranger in that hostelry's common room, however, was not difficult. Ridley proved a personable fellow, if somewhat rigid in his beliefs. He also struck Nick as being deeply troubled.

"In town for the Assizes?" Nick asked him.

"In a manner of speaking."

"I've a civil suit pending."

"My employer sent me to Maidstone. I'd not have come else. I take no pleasure in being here." Brooding, he drank deeply from his tankard, then looked more closely at Nick. "I have seen you before. Near the gaol. You appeared to be waiting for someone."

To delay his answer, Nick took a turn to drink deep. The same instinct that had made him a successful merchant told him Ridley was an honest man who would respond to the truth but meet evasive answers with silence. "I waited there for Lady Appleton to come out," he admitted. "I believe you know the gentlewoman."

Momentary surprise flickered in Ridley's expressive

eyes. "Aye, but I have no notion why she should interest herself in Mistress Crane's plight."

"Mistress Crane did not tell you?"

"Mistress Crane would prefer not to speak to me at all, let alone answer any questions I pose."

Something in his tone made Nick wonder if there was more to the clergyman's interest in Constance Crane than the concern of chaplain for parishioner. He put that intriguing thought aside to contemplate later and instead gave Ridley part of the answer to his question.

"They had friends in common when Lady Appleton was in the household of the duke of Northumberland and Mistress Crane served the marchioness of Northampton."

"I see." It was clear he did not.

"I do not believe they had spoken since before Lady Northampton's death but when Lady Appleton heard Mistress Crane's name, she wished to know if the accused witch was the same woman."

"Vulgar curiosity?" Ridley inquired.

Nick shrugged. He hesitated to tell Ridley that Susanna Appleton was committed to the pursuit of justice. Such an uncommon passion in a woman might too easily be misinterpreted. When the charge was witchcraft, it was wise to take no chances.

"Does she believe Constance . . . Mistress Crane?"

"I think she does," Nick said cautiously. "Is it so impossible for the woman to be innocent?"

Ridley drank again. He sighed. He stared at his hands where they were clasped around the tankard. "I would like to believe she did no wrong. I would like to believe she never took Peter Marsh into her bed."

"Mayhap she did not. Unless you caught them there . . ."

"There was something between them."

"Who was this Marsh she's accused of killing?"

"He served in the household at Mill Hall before I came there."

"In what position?"

"Clerk. When Hugo Garrard decided to install his own chaplain, he assigned Marsh's tasks to me and let him go."

"Then if it had been you beneath that tree, Marsh would have been the obvious suspect."

Smiling at Ridley's horrified reaction to this suggestion, Nick signaled for more beer.

14

On a morning that was near perfect, Susanna and Jennet set out again from Mill Hall, this time on foot. A faint blue haze had hung over the countryside at dawn, but it had soon been dispersed by the breeze blowing inland from the sea, a bracing current of air that carried the invigorating tang of salt air and the sweet scent of thyme.

Susanna paused to look south over level marshland. Across a landscape brilliant with juniper bushes, fritillaries, harebells, and scabious, she caught a glimpse of the Narrow Sea, its salt water glistening in the distance.

"I am told the edge of that inland cliff once marked the coastline," she told Jennet, nodding toward the promontory. "Then the sea receded and created Romney Marsh."

At supper the previous night, Hugo Garrard had responded with monosyllabic answers to her questions about his cousins, but later he had been somewhat more forthcoming on the subject of Mill Hall and its environs. What had once been shoreline, he'd told her, was now anywhere from a quarter to half a mile from the sea. Mudbanks and a great buildup of shingle had added to the land, filling in harbors. Where once ships could have sailed right up to the foot of a hill, now it was surrounded by marshland. As if to repay the inhabitants for the loss of convenient shipping, in time this came to provide a most luxuriant feeding ground for cattle. Grass grew in abundance hereabout.

The footpath was wide enough to allow Susanna and Jennet to walk side by side. As they followed it, the cries of gulls and guillemots faded, replaced by the song of a yellowhammer. Soon they came to a small chapel built of golden gray sandstone that gleamed in the sun. Two gigantic elms rose one on either side, each higher than the spire.

"A remote spot for a house of worship," Jennet remarked.

"When it was built, this area was more populous. There are Roman ruins atop that rise." She pointed to the ancient walls, only just visible from their vantage point. They were lost from view when the trail meandered into a small wood.

Trees clustered thick around them, ivy clinging to many of the trunks. Here and there roots were exposed, some of their gnarled surfaces big enough to sit upon.

Jennet kept glancing back over her shoulder. When they surprised a squirrel, causing it to dash across the path and into the underbrush, she let out a little squeak of alarm.

"We should have brought Fulke and Lionel along," she mumbled.

"Why?"

"This is an evil place, full of ghosts and witches. And there are smugglers, too."

"Smugglers I will believe. And no doubt they are the ones who've spread rumors of ghosts and witches, the better to keep curious folk away."

Jennet chewed on her lower lip as she contemplated whether to accept the logic of this argument. She said no more until the path descended into a rectangular clearing. They had reached Lucy Milborne's cottage.

"Are you certain this is the right dwelling?"

Susanna could understand her confusion. What everyone had called a cottage was in truth a substantial black-and-white timber-frame farmhouse with an upper story.

Before entering, she surveyed the lay of the land. There was only one wych elm in sight. It stood less than a bowshot from the door, but the ground beneath it was obscured from sight by a heavy growth of bushes. It was possible that a body might have lain under this tree and not have been seen by anyone at the cottage . . . unless they chanced to glance out an upper window.

Had Peter Marsh been there while Constance and Lucy dug in Lucy's garden? Susanna also had to wonder if he had arrived alive or had been put in place after he was already dead.

The door to the cottage was not locked.

Two rooms, linked by a passage, ran the length of the north side. If anyone before them had been in to look at Lucy's possessions, they had taken care not to disturb anything. The authorities, Susanna thought, might have decided to rely upon the examination of witnesses. Others would have been put off by their own superstitious fear.

Moving through the lower level, she came to the well-equipped stillroom in a separate building at the back, next to the herb garden Constance had told them about. Susanna examined both, then reentered the house to climb to the upper story, pausing on the landing to note that the window there did not face the wych elm. What she could just make out over the tops of the surrounding trees was the spire of the chapel they had passed and the chimneys of Mill Hall on the high ground beyond.

At her mistress's heels, Jennet continued to grumble to herself. Susanna heard her mutter something about a "street of demons" but ignored this obscure reference in favor of exploring Lucy's bedchamber. It had its own fireplace and a comfortable feather bed, a chair, and several storage chests. A brief search of the contents of the latter revealed no incriminating evidence—no wax poppets, no pentagrams, no human bones . . . and no books or papers. There had been none in the stillroom, either, which struck Susanna as passing strange. Had someone been here, after all, and seized any writings and books? Or had Lucy managed to secrete them somewhere before her arrest?

A speculative gleam in her eyes, Susanna studied the hearth more closely. Was there a hiding place concealed behind the stones? She'd heard of fireplaces constructed with secret compartments big enough to hold a man. She was about to cross the room and test the stones for looseness when Jennet, at the window, gasped out her name.

"What is it?"

"There is a man under the wych elm."

Susanna discovered she had been right. From this height, one might have been able to see a dead body lying beneath the tree. Jennet's man, however, was very much alive, lounging against the trunk and staring back at them.

She took her time studying him. A young man, somewhere in his early twenties. He was so slender as to be almost skeletal, that build emphasized by his excessive height. She shifted her attention to his face and concluded she had never seen him before. Lank, straw-colored hair framed features notable for a nose that looked as if it had been broken at least once. He was clean shaven but would, Susanna decided, have looked better with a beard.

To her amusement, her scrutiny seemed to discomfit the stranger. As she continued to assess him, a dull red tide swept up into his cheeks.

"Let us go down and see what he wants," she said to Jennet.

"He's trouble," Jennet predicted.

"Good morrow, sirrah," Susanna greeted him when they reached the wych elm.

Having recovered his composure, he doffed his cap. "Lady Appleton, I presume?"

At the sound of his voice, Jennet went stiff.

"You have the advantage of me," Susanna said, "but not, I do think, of my companion."

"You are the one who accosted me last night." Hands on her hips, Jennet glared at him. "He is the one who told me this place was near the Street of Demons, and that it was haunted."

"And has he a name?"

"Not that he revealed to me."

They both looked at the stranger, expectant.

Through murky green eyes, he stared warily back.

"Well?" Susanna demanded.

"Norden. Chediok Norden." Once he decided to speak, the young man's words flowed forth in such a rush that he stumbled over them, then turned scarlet as a cardinal's robes. "I am here to learn the truth about Mother Milborne and Mistress Crane."

"What are they to you?" Susanna asked.

He stammered his answer. "Bread and butter."

"Young man, I am not going to beat you, bewitch you, or berate you. Do me the courtesy of giving me a coherent answer to my question. Who are you and why are you here?"

Swallowing hard, he managed a cocky smile at odds

with his nervousness. "I am a scribbler, madam. A writer of verses and pamphlets."

That was direct enough, but scarce pleasing to her.

"What manner of pamphlet?" She suspected she already knew.

"Accounts of trials."

As she'd feared.

These small books, printed in quarto and unbound, were produced by the thousands in London and sold for a penny to satisfy a voracious public appetite for scandal. They were hawked in the streets, along with almanacs full of prognostications and broadside ballads containing the dying words of penitent sinners about to be executed for their crimes.

Typeset in bold black ink and illustrated with woodcuts, they were so popular that they sometimes made their way into the country, even though only a few petty chapmen wished to be bothered carrying them. A quarto was an awkward size to fit into a peddler's pack. The one that had reached Leigh Abbey in April had both delighted and terrified the entire household.

Out of duty, being responsible for their moral character, Susanna had begun to read it. Once started, she'd felt compelled to go on, all the way to the end, even as she'd despised herself for wanting to know more. She was unable to explain the bizarre fascination the text had exerted over her.

The author, who'd signed his versified introduction with the name John Philip, appeared to have been present at the Essex Assizes the previous summer, when three witches had been tried and found guilty at Chelmsford.

To her sorrow, Susanna was all too familiar with the workings of the law. Even before she'd opened the pamphlet, she'd wondered how much of the tale Master Philip had invented to attract buyers for his prose.

The more she'd read, the more convinced she'd become that his was a largely fictional narrative, rather than the "true relation" it claimed to be.

Actual events might have inspired the story, and the trial could have included some of the incidents Philip claimed, but she doubted it had been filled with as much innuendo and outright slander as were related in the pamphlet. In particular, she thought the amorous exploits of the accused were unlikely to have been taken up at their trial.

"In other words," she now said to Norden, "you mean to exploit the accusations against Mistress Milborne and Mistress Crane for your own profit."

"Nay, madam. I perform a public service. I write only the truth." Once again, he spoke too rapidly and stumbled over the last word.

"Hah!" This from Jennet.

"And what is the truth?"

Norden's Adam's apple wobbled before he got control of himself. "That these two women are witches." He lowered his voice and leaned closer to Susanna. "Both women kept cats. Familiars."

"I saw no sign of one in Lucy's house."

There had been a cat, Sathan, in the Chelmsford case. According to Master Philip, a woman named Mother Eve had given this cat to her granddaughter, Elizabeth Francis, who kept him for many years before passing him on to one Mother Waterhouse. Calculating the figures Philip gave, Susanna had come to the astonishing conclusion that this cat must have reached the age of four and twenty. He was also said to have turned himself, on separate occasions, into a dog and into a toad. A most remarkable beast.

" 'Tis said Mistress Crane told her familiar to touch Peter Marsh's body," Norden related in an earnest voice. "When it did so, Marsh fell down dead with no mark upon him."

Something very like that had happened, at least according to Master Philip's pamphlet, in Chelmsford. Frowning, Susanna glanced at Jennet, who looked as if she, too, had been struck by the similarity.

"Who says this?" Susanna asked Norden.

"Why . . . everyone. They say—"

"They? I know not this 'they' and trust those gossips even less. You repeat rumor, sirrah. I demand proof. Where is this cat you speak of? Produce it."

"Doubtless it turned itself into a bird and flew away, else it should have been arrested with its mistress."

"More likely it never existed at all."

"Then how did Marsh die? He was found just here, beneath this tree."

Susanna looked up into the branches over her head. The wych elm was very large but in no other way extraordinary. Next she surveyed the bushes surrounding it and for a moment her heart constricted. She could not fail to recognize them. Banewort grew throughout Kent, its coal black berries tempting the unwary to taste them.

Many years ago, Susanna's sister had eaten just a few of those shiny fruits. She'd been dead in a matter of hours.

"How did Peter Marsh look when he was found?" she asked Norden. "Was his body contorted with pain? Were his limbs straight or did he lie curled into himself?"

"They say . . ." He stopped himself and began again. "The constable who came to examine the body told me that he lay sprawled on his face on the ground, that he looked as if he had been picked up by the scruff of the neck and dropped by a giant hand."

"Who found the body?"

He hesitated. "I am told it was Mistress Damascin Edgecumbe, the daughter of old Clement, the man Mother Milborne did bewitch to death."

An interesting coincidence, Susanna thought. When she spoke, her tone was critical. "You are told, you say. Did you not speak to the woman yourself?"

"Not with her dragon of a mother on guard."

"Just how well do you know the people of this area?"

His color heightened once more as he mumbled, "I dwell in London."

For the nonce, Susanna let the evasive reply stand. She turned to Jennet. "We must go on to Edgecumbe Manor at once. It should be just beyond those trees." She indicated a break in the woods at the far side of the clearing, the point where the track she and Jennet had been following resumed.

A visit to Lucy's neighbors had been the next logical step in her investigation, although she'd originally meant to complete her search of the cottage before going on. That would have to wait for the return journey. She felt a sudden, urgent need to first discover the details of Clement Edgecumbe's last hours.

"If you follow the footpath," Norden said, confirming the directions Susanna had received at Mill Hall, "you will reach the manor house in less than a quarter of an hour."

The distance between the two estates, she realized, was comparable to that between Leigh Abbey and Whitethorn Manor.

She expected Norden to come with them, but when she looked back through the thick growth of elm and beech, he was nowhere in sight. She shrugged off her sense of unease. If Norden had wanted to search Lucy's cottage, he could have done so at any time. She continued on, Jennet at her heels.

By its style of architecture and the choice of building

material, Edgecumbe Manor looked to have been constructed sometime within the last thirty years. White stone alternated with the glossy faces of split flint to make a distinctive checkered pattern.

"A goodly house," she murmured.

"Aye. And a busy one." Jennet indicated the kitchen yard, where two huge copper cauldrons and a bucking tub had been set up. "Laundry day. One of the two big washes of the year, if I am any judge of such things."

A few minutes later, standing beside the bucking tub used to wash sheets and tablecloths, Susanna got her first look at Mildred Edgecumbe. To work with her women, Clement's widow had put on an old gown of Naples fustian. Her hair was completely covered by a wimple, which served to accent piercing gray eyes. These grew ever more wary as she listened to Susanna's apologies for intruding on her unannounced.

After talking to Hugo, Susanna had decided she'd have better luck extracting information from the Edgecumbes if she did not present herself as Constance's defender. She affected an incredulous, somewhat addlepated manner and gushed at Mildred.

"Constance Crane was an intimate friend of my late husband's family. We were most distressed to hear the news of her arrest and I felt I must go straight to dear Hugo to find out if it was true."

Mildred gave a disdainful sniff. " 'Tis true. No doubt of it. He'll have told you so. Why come to me?"

"To hear of it firsthand. Will you disclose what you know to me, that I may understand how Mistress Crane came to such a pass?"

Uncertain what to make of such a request, Mildred put her off. "You will have to wait. The water has been drained and it is time to pour in the lye." She nodded toward the bucking tub, which perched on a stand raised a foot off the ground. Linen, Susanna knew, had to be folded and placed inside in a precise manner that ensured water would flow freely around it. She wondered if Mildred's women used sticks to hold apart the bundles, as Susanna's grandmother had taught her to do.

Getting a whiff of the strong solution, Susanna wrinkled her nose. She retreated a few feet. There would be opportunity for questions after the lye had been added and the linens were left to soak.

"A long, tiresome process," Jennet remarked as they watched servants scurry to obey their mistress's exacting orders. "Rinse and soak. Drain. Turn. Rearrange. Rinse in running water. Even then the job is not done. Wet linens must be spread out on the ground or over bushes to be bleached in sun. And wetted down. And bleached again. And then—"

"Enough." Susanna had never had a great deal of interest in such domestic duties and was happy to let Jennet supervise them at Leigh Abbey. Her passions were her herb garden and the business of running her estate. She was happiest in her stillroom and in the study where she kept accounts and records.

That did not mean she was ignorant of what went on in her laundry. She had been taught how to clean clothing and linens, just as she had been instructed in the rudiments of embroidery and sewing a garment. That she avoided all such dull chores whenever possible did not mean she could not call upon dozens of half-forgotten skills, but only if it became necessary to do so.

While they waited for Mildred, a young woman came out into the kitchen yard. Tears flowing down her cheeks, she held a gown clasped to her bosom.

"Mother," she wailed. "I cannot get this stain out of the velvet."

So this was Damascin, the one Norden claimed had found Marsh's body. Susanna studied her with critical eyes. She could be no more than twenty and had a delicate prettiness Susanna supposed would make her attractive to men despite the whine in her voice. Long, blond hair flowed down her back in ostentatious proclamation that she was an unwed, innocent virgin.

"Use the pot with the mertum cudum," her mother instructed. "Wash the spot in it and let it dry in the sun."

Startled into a protest, Susanna found herself the focus of every eye and perforce was obliged to explain her outburst. "The compound you suggest contains raw red arsenic, a poison. Use too much and there may be unfortunate consequences. The juice of soapwort, left on a spot for one hour, washed with clean water, reapplied, then washed out with lukewarm water will produce the same result with less hazard to the health."

"And how do you know so much about it?" Mildred demanded.

"She wrote a book on poisons," Jennet bragged before Susanna could stop her. " 'Tis called *A Cautionary Herbal.*"

Susanna had not intended to make that known, given what she'd seen at the wych elm. Arsenic, since it did not come from a plant, had not even been included in her herbal. But the damage was done now. She kept silent.

"Well," Mildred Edgecumbe said to her daughter, "you heard Lady Appleton. Go and use soapwort."

The young woman scurried back into the house.

Susanna started after her. "I can show her how—"

"No. Leave her be. My daughter has had a difficult time of it. I'll not have her badgered."

"I've no intention—"

"If you have questions, ask them of me."

A dragon indeed, Susanna thought, and abandoned her earlier pretense. 'Very well. Tell me how Lucy Milborne caused your husband's death."

"She bewitched him."

"You will need to be more specific, madam."

Apparently sensing that Susanna would not give up until she had heard the entire story, Mildred first took a moment to give further instructions to her servants, then drew her uninvited guest aside, into the shelter of a rose arbor, and launched into an account so clipped that it sounded as if she had learned it by rote. She did not notice that Jennet had sidled up behind her to listen.

"Lucy Milborne had a familiar. She bade it do her evil deeds for her. Every time it carried out a task, she rewarded it with a drop of her own blood. She pricked herself, sometimes in one place and sometimes in another, and where she pricked, there remained for some time a red spot, for her familiar did suckle it like a woman's teat, drawing blood rather than milk."

Susanna felt her eyes widen at this absurd claim, but she did not interrupt.

"The first time we knew of it was when my husband went to put on his shoe of a morning and found a creature much like a toad lying inside it. He touched it with his foot and he was forthwith taken with a lameness whereof he could not be healed."

"The familiar was a toad?"

"A familiar can take what shape it will. Another time it was a cat. It sat on Lucy Milborne's lap and she told it to kill three of our hogs, which it did, and she rewarded it as I have told you."

"But your husband's death, madam, how can that—"

"She had a falling out with Clement and willed her

familiar to kill him. A few days later, he fell into a dead sleep from which he never woke."

Tears came into the widow's eyes. Preposterous as this story was, she seemed to believe it. "And then Lucy Milborne rewarded the foul creature," Mildred added on a heartwrenching sob. "Rewarded it as I have told you, with her own blood. There can be no possible doubt about it, Lady Appleton. That woman is a witch."

15

Jennet believed witches had supernatural powers, accepted that a person could be both bewitched and unwitched. But Mildred Edgecumbe's account of her husband's death bore more than a passing resemblance to the charges made the previous year against a Chelmsford woman named Elizabeth Francis. Indeed, everything Mistress Milborne and Mistress Crane had been accused of echoed the story told in the pamphlet Jennet had bought from a passing chapman.

"Your husband was not bewitched, Mistress Edgecumbe," Lady Appleton said. "Poisoned, mayhap, but not bewitched."

Taken aback, Mildred Edgecumbe sputtered heated words. "What effrontery! How dare you contradict me?"

Her servants stopped to stare, although they were quick to resume their work when their mistress rounded on them with a quelling glare. Jennet slipped into a better spot from which to listen. When Mistress Edgecumbe turned back to Lady Appleton, Jennet had a clear view of a face suffused with annoyance.

"Listen to me," Lady Appleton begged. "You do much wrong an innocent woman if you persist in your claims."

A calculating expression replaced the look of irritation in Mistress Edgecumbe's cold gray eyes. "Poison, you say? What poison? And if you are correct in your assumption, what is to say it was not Lucy Milborne who poisoned Clement?"

"Tell me first about the period just before your husband died," Lady Appleton countered. "Did he have difficulty speaking? Complain of numbness in his limbs?"

"He was found in the barn, already unconscious and unmoving."

Lady Appleton looked past the widow, raised her voice, and addressed the servants. "Did no one see him before he fell into the dead sleep?"

Jennet had no doubt most of the women had overheard every word their betters had exchanged.

"Edmund the stableboy did," one laundress volunteered, braving Mistress Edgecumbe's wrath. "Told us he was all wild-eyed and raving. Made him afeared."

"This Edmund—where is he? I would speak with him at once.

"Lady Appleton," Mistress Edgecumbe interrupted, "I find your demands and your behavior offensive."

"I find murder offensive, Mistress Edgecumbe. As your husband lay unconscious, could you hear his heart beating as if it would burst out of his chest? Was his skin hot and dry to the touch? And ruddy?"

Although she gave no verbal answer, Mildred Edgecumbe's eyes betrayed her. Lady Appleton's words had hit their mark, Jennet thought. Clement Edgecumbe had exhibited at least one of those symptoms.

"Think about what I have said," Lady Appleton urged. "It will be too late to change your mind once the women now in Maidstone gaol have been executed."

"If you do not leave of your own volition, Lady Appleton, I will order my menservants to force you to go."

Jennet feared her mistress might persist, if only to see if the stableboy might be among the henchmen Mistress Edgecumbe summoned to evict her. But after a moment, Lady Appleton accepted temporary defeat, bade the other woman a polite farewell, and began to retrace her steps through the kitchen yard.

Caught off guard by the abrupt retreat, Jennet was some distance behind her mistress. As she left her place of concealment and followed, she saw two laundresses lift a steaming cauldron from the flames. At the very moment Lady Appleton passed the bucking tub, they began to pour.

Boiling water sloshed hard against the wooden interior of the heavy tub. An instant later, the stand beneath it collapsed. Before Jennet's horrified gaze, the contents, a dangerous mixture of lye and scalding water, spewed forth—straight toward Lady Appleton.

16

Jennet's scream gave Susanna warning. She leapt aside, avoiding the worst of the danger, but she fell in her frantic effort to get out of the way. She landed on her knees with enough force to elicit a cry. Then that pain was forgotten as her right hand, flung out as she attempted to break her fall, was engulfed by a burning flood. She jerked it back, but it was too late. The damage had been done.

Better one hand than her entire body, she told herself, staring at the rapidly reddening skin. As her mind struggled to cope with the shock of being scalded, she could almost hear her grandmother's voice, telling her she'd regret it one day if she did not behave like a gentlewoman. True gentlewomen always wore gloves. And hats. If the day had not been so warm, or if they'd ridden to Edgecumbe Manor, Susanna would have been wearing gloves. They'd have protected her from the worst of the damage.

"Madam?"

Jennet's anxious voice brought Susanna back to the present. The back of her hand felt as if it were on fire.

"Let me see your injury, madam. Are you burnt elsewhere? One side of your skirt is soaked."

So it was, but the only hurt Susanna felt in her legs

came from bruised knees. With Jennet's help, she stumbled to her feet.

Mildred Edgecumbe was all contrition now, trying to hustle Susanna into the house and fussing about what to put on the burn. "You shall have a kirtle from mine own wardrobe to replace your drenched clothing," she declared.

"That is the least of my concerns," Susanna told her. "Jennet, find a house leek. The juice will soothe mine hand." She was unwilling to trust Mildred's remedies but did accept a medicinal cup of aqua vitae.

Following treatment, Susanna's skin felt less painful and upon inspection she saw that the damage was not as bad as she'd first feared. No blisters were forming.

She would have been in far worse condition, she realized, had Jennet not warned her in time. Boiling water or lye alone could do considerable harm, especially the latter, in particular if it had gotten into her eyes. Together they might have caused permanent damage. And if the heavy bucking tub had struck her . . .

Susanna made her excuses as soon as she felt steady enough to walk back to Mill Hall. She declined the offer of dry clothing. Neither Mildred Edgecumbe's garments nor her daughter's would have fit her.

Damascin had not reappeared, but Susanna felt no inclination to stay longer in the hope of questioning her. Not with Mildred hovering like a mother hen over her chick. Assuring the woman that she bore her no ill-will on account of the accident, insisting her injury was nothing to be concerned about, she made her escape.

Jennet hurried after her. "How bad is your injury? Are you certain you can walk so far?"

"I do not walk on my hands."

"Was it an accident?" Jennet asked.

Susanna narrowed her eyes, slanting a look in Jennet's direction as they entered the forest. "Did you see anything to indicate otherwise?"

" 'Twas . . . convenient," Jennet pointed out. "You asked questions. Raised doubts."

"All is not as it seems at Edgecumbe Manor, but I do not think my questions could have been enough to provoke someone to attempt murder."

"If they poisoned Master Edgecumbe—"

"How could anyone arrange for a bucking tub to collapse? I suppose that either Mistress Edgecumbe or her daughter might have given orders to stage such a mishap, but it seems an uncertain method."

"Unless their real goal was to do you in by poison when they treated your burns."

"God's teeth, Jennet! You try my patience."

Jennet looked startled, as well she should be, for on the rare occasion when Susanna was driven to profanity, her usual curse was a mild "Bodykins!" Worse, "God's teeth!" had been one of Robert Appleton's favorite oaths.

"My injury makes my temper short," Susanna apologized. "And I am more annoyed with myself than with you. I, too, let my imagination run wild. I should have remained long enough to speak with Damascin. And with that stableboy, Edmund. I should have used this hand as an excuse." Clearly, the pain had addled her wits.

"Go back tomorrow, madam, if you must. For now, you need to rest and recover."

"At least my accident gives us an excuse to stay at Mill Hall for a second night, time enough to think of a good reason to return to Edgecumbe Manor on the morrow." She increased her pace, anxious to get back to Lucy's cottage.

Chediok Norden was nowhere in sight when Susanna

and Jennet reached the wych elm. Susanna wanted to speak to him again, too, but for the moment was glad both clearing and cottage were deserted.

"There is a salve in the stillroom that will soothe my hand," she told Jennet. "A treatment for burns that I noticed when we were there earlier."

"You would trust a witch's recipe?"

"Sooner than Mildred Edgecumbe's. And this salve is one with which I am familiar." The ingredients had been listed on a neatly printed label: plantain and daisy leaves, the green bark of elders, and green germanders. Lucy had no doubt stamped them all together with oil and strained the result through linen cloth to make a soothing ointment.

Susanna located the ceramic pot and applied a liberal coat of Lucy's balm to her injured flesh. She slipped the little container into the pocket hidden in a placket in her kirtle for future treatments, although she had medicines of her own making in the capcase she carried whenever she traveled. Among them were her daily tonic, ginger for seasickness, lettuce cakes to treat insomnia, the expressed juice of adder's-tongue leaves for sore eyes, and an all-purpose salve that served for sores and abrasions as well as burns—a mixture of comfrey, St. John's wort, calendula, plantain, and oil of lavender. It did not do to leave home unprepared.

"Madam, you need rest," Jennet protested when Susanna entered the cottage instead of setting out at once for Mill Hall.

"I need your help here first, Jennet. I believe the fireplace in Lucy's bedchamber contains a secret compartment. With your two good hands and my one, we must search for it."

Diverted by the promise of a treasure hunt, Jennet ceased her objections. They soon found what they were looking for—a leather bag hidden inside a deep, square hole behind a loose stone at eye level. Jennet fumbled with the drawstring that held it closed, then dropped the contents into Susanna's uninjured hand.

"What is it? Jewelry?"

Susanna studied the object and wondered why she should be surprised. "It is a rosary."

"Lucy Milborne is a secret Papist?"

"More than that. There could be other reasons to have a rosary of this distinctive type, but the simplest seems most likely. At some time before King Henry dissolved the monasteries, Lucy Milborne was a nun."

17

Money was a useful thing. The day after Susanna left for Mill Hall, Nick Baldwin had in his hands a copy of "An Act against Conjurations, Enchantments, and Witchcrafts." That afternoon, he closed himself into the parlor of his house in Maidstone and studied the text of the statute as carefully as a schoolboy preparing a Latin recitation.

What he read disturbed him.

It was not that he disagreed with the biblical strictures insisting that a witch should be killed. He was as religious as the next man and knew there were no fewer than three instances, in Exodus, Leviticus, and Deuteronomy, that insisted upon this punishment. But this law, which had gone into effect on the first of June four years earlier, did not simply address the crime of bewitching a man to death. It included as witchcraft a broad range of practices, some of which did not seem to Nick to be either criminal or heretical.

In addition, after his conversation with Adrian Ridley, Nick had realized that many of those who took it upon themselves to pursue witches in England had been infected by the same mania that drove witch hunters in southern Europe. Men like the Reverend Thomas Cole would not be satisfied with finding one or two unfortunate women and hanging them. They expected to discover large numbers of evildoers and prosecute them all.

That they would find them, one way or another, troubled Nick. After three tankards of beer, Ridley had regaled the patrons of The Ship with the tale of how forty witches had been rounded up and burnt all together at Toulouse.

Everything he heard and read increased Nick's fears for Susanna. If she continued to interest herself in Constance Crane, and he knew her too well to think she could be persuaded to desist, she could make herself a target for the witch hunters. On her return to Maidstone, with or without an alternative explanation for Peter Marsh's sudden death, she would doubtless argue for Constance's release, thus bringing herself to the attention of Cole and his ilk. If these men learned that her particular area of expertise was poisonous herbs, they would assume the worst.

Nick now knew better than to hope Susanna's status as a gentlewoman would provide any protection. According to Ridley, even noblewomen could be executed for witchcraft.

Kneading both fists into his burning eyes, Nick tried to think. Somehow, he must protect her. Was there a spell against suspicion? He supposed not, else most of those accused of crimes, the guilty as well as the innocent, would have made use of it.

With a sigh, he concluded that the starting place must be a thorough familiarity with the law. As he read through the statute yet again, he took notes.

The charges used to arrest Mistress Crane and Mistress Milborne were clear enough. They had "used and practiced witch crafts, enchantments, charms, and sorceries to the destruction of the persons and goods of their neighbors and other subjects of this realm, and for other lewd intents and purposes contrary to the laws of Almighty God, to the peril of their own souls and to the great infamy and disquietness of this realm."

The statute went on to say that those who bewitched another to death must be tried as felons and executed, without benefit of sanctuary or clergy. There was one concession made in cases of witchcraft. The estates of other sorts of convicted felons were forfeit but the heirs of an executed witch might still inherit land and titles and other rights, as if no such attainder had been made.

Nick wondered what person stood to gain all Constance Crane possessed. Who was Lucy Milborne's heir? Both women were gently born, but Ridley had told him that they lived on the charity of their cousin Hugo. Constance earned her keep by managing the household at Mill Hall. Lucy's cottage stood at the very edge of the land belonging to the demesne farm.

At least, Nick thought, it was unlikely anyone would accuse Susanna of bewitching another person to death. Nor had she much to fear under the second provision in the law, which dealt with causing another, or that person's goods or cattle, to be damaged. Those convicted of this crime were imprisoned for a year for a first offense, without bail or mainprise, and once every quarter were taken to the market on market day and put in the pillory for the space of six hours, during which time they had to openly confess their error and offense.

Those who survived a year in gaol should have learned their lesson, he thought, and to give them further incentive to refrain from casting spells, the punishment for a second offense was death.

No, Susanna had little to fear from either of those two accusations under the new law, but the third provision worried him. It was illegal to use witchcraft for purposes that could also be achieved without supernatural assistance. As he had already warned Susanna, even a healer could stand accused under this provision. As could those who showed a talent for finding lost or stolen objects.

These were "enchantments," as was using witchcraft to find treasure or to provoke unlawful love. All were punished by imprisonment for a year for a first offense. A second offense resulted in life imprisonment and the forfeiture of all goods and cattle. That might as well be a death sentence, Nick thought. Even a year could be fatal. Disease killed many prisoners. Others went mad.

Nick was pulled from these dismal ponderings by the sound of horses' hooves on cobblestones. His first thought was that Susanna had returned. He told himself it was just possible, if she'd found the answers she sought at Mill Hall the previous evening and set out at first light this morning.

Rising, he crossed the room to the semioctagonal bay window that took up most of one end of the house. It overlooked his stable. When Nick leaned out, a smile split his face. A woman in widow's weeds led the newly arrived riders.

But a moment later, his expression turned to dismay.

That was not Susanna in his courtyard.

It was his mother.

18

Hugo Garrard was not at home when Jennet and her mistress returned to Mill Hall. Since he no longer had a housekeeper, Constance Crane having been forcibly removed from that position, Jennet encountered little difficulty with Master Garrard's servants. They would stay a second night, she'd told them in her firmest voice. No one had dared object.

After she had applied more salve to Lady Appleton's poor abused hand, using a feather to anoint the tender, scarlet-hued tissue, and daubed some on her bruised and scraped knees, as well, Jennet tucked her mistress into bed for the rest she sorely needed if she was to recuperate. Lady Appleton resisted at first, insisting there were questions she must have answers to. Only by promising she would ask them did Jennet persuade Lady Appleton to stay put.

As her first stop, Jennet invaded the kitchen, a fine big room with a flagged floor that sloped down to the drains to allow waste water to be carried off. There she found the cook, a robust individual with a stony countenance, supervising two underlings, a kitchen maid and a scullion, in the selection of foodstuffs for supper.

Jennet belatedly realized she had missed dinner by accompanying Lady Appleton on her sojourn to Lucy's cottage and Edgecumbe Manor. The lingering smells of fresh baked bread and roasting meat made her mouth water.

Cook appeared to have a soft spot for wounded creatures. A dog with a broken leg, carefully splinted, slept on a pallet near the hearth. Jennet explained about Lady Appleton's accident.

"How does the poor lady now?" Cook asked.

"Burns are painful."

His rueful laugh told her he knew that from personal experience. "Aye. A pity old Mother Milborne was tooken away. She had a salve—"

"Lady Appleton stopped at the cottage on her way back here to retrieve it."

He nodded his approval.

Jennet awaited further comment. She had not a doubt in the world that every servant at Mill Hall knew Lady Appleton was there on Mistress Crane's behalf.

Cook said only, "I will give you a strengthening broth to take to her when she wakes, and make her a flommary caudle, too."

"I'd not mind something to eat myself." Jennet's stomach growled to emphasize the fact that she'd missed a meal.

Cook was not in as much sympathy with her, since she had no visible wounds, but when he had mixed a goodly quantity of ale with wine and tipped in a few spoonfuls of wheat bran seasoned with sugar and orange-flower water, he added a second helping. Without a word, he divided the caudle into two portions, putting one in a mazer which he handed to Jennet.

While she devoured this offering with ill-concealed greed, he continued with what he'd been doing when she interrupted him, inspecting the contents of several storage barrels to make sure he had adequate supplies.

The twice-annual trip to Maidstone for the Assizes was also an opportunity to restock provisions.

One large barrel, Jennet saw, held dried fish, another olives, and a third dried fruit. All were less than half full. When she had polished off the contents of the mazer, Jennet examined some of the smaller storage containers.

"Sweetmeats in that wooden box," Cook said, relenting yet again. "You may help yourself to one. But no more than that, mind."

Jennet took him up on the offer, then peeked into a straight-sided earthenware jug with a rim, hoping for some sort of preserves. It held only clarified butter for cooking.

"Is there aught else you want?" It was plain Cook did not approve of her wandering to and fro, poking amongst things that were none of her concern.

A great deal, Jennet thought, but she supposed it would do no good to come right out and ask what Lady Appleton wished to know.

"You have a goodly household here," Jennet began, hoping she sounded innocently admiring. She had been delegated to discover what those who had dealt with Mistress Crane on a daily basis had thought of her . . . before she'd been charged with being a witch. "A personal chaplain, too, I hear."

"Aye."

"That fellow who was found under the wych elm—did he not work here, too?"

"I'll speak no ill of the dead." The flat finality in the cook's voice warned Jennet that he did not intend to volunteer any information about Peter Marsh.

Tiring quickly of her effort at subtlety, Jennet gave it up in favor of posing a direct question. "Do you think Mistress Crane killed him?"

As if reciting a lesson, Cook repeated the same stories Jennet had heard before . . . in almost the exact same words. The mistress ill-used and abandoned. The kneeling in the garden. The revenge. Every time she heard the tale, Jennet believed it less.

But this time there was one new detail. It had been, Cook said, Arthur Kennison who claimed to have overheard the two witches chanting to their master, the devil.

"In the herb garden, they were," he repeated. "On their knees. He saw them there hissel."

Arthur Kennison. Jennet remembered what Mistress Crane had said of him. He'd passed by at a distance on the morning of the day on which Peter Marsh had been found dead. The morning she and her cousin had been working in the garden after spending half the night in the woods gathering some heathen herb.

"Why would he make such a claim?"

"Because 'tis true." Cook gave her a contemptuous look. "The obvious answer," she agreed. This interrogation was not progressing the way she'd hoped. She dawdled over eating the sweetmeat she'd selected.

The dog stirred in its sleep, emitting a sound that was half groan and half snore, reminding Jennet of another matter about which Lady Appleton was curious. She wanted to know if Mistress Crane had kept a cat, or any other creature that might be mistaken for a familiar. She was convinced that Mistress Milborne had not.

"Are there other animals about?" Jennet asked, nodding toward the sleeping hound.

"Another dog or two, for hunting. A ferret to keep the rats down."

He did not mention cats. Or toads. "Lady Appleton's sister-by-marriage kept a ferret as a pet," Jennet remarked. "Nasty beast. Always biting."

Cook did not respond. Instead he ordered the scullion to get busy chopping turnips and handed a wicker basket to the maidservant, Emma by name, dispatching her to the kitchen garden to pick parsley.

Jennet left the kitchen soon afterward.

Emma looked terrified when Jennet approached her. She was a mouse of a girl, all big teeth and pock-marked skin. Jennet sent a reassuring smile in her direction and began to help with the parsley, adding one or two more sprigs to those already in the basket.

"You have nothing to fear from me, Emma," she said after a moment. "I am only here in search of a fresh house leek for my mistress's burn."

Knowing it would take a concerted effort to put Emma at her ease, Jennet started talking. If she left the girl with the false impression that she was nothing more than Lady Appleton's tiring maid, why, 'twas in a good cause. With infinite patience, Jennet persevered. At last, just as she despaired of success, Emma ventured a comment.

"She was a good mistress."

"Mistress Crane?"

"Aye." And with that, Emma began to talk freely.

Luck ran Lady Appleton's way at last. Emma, Jennet learned, had been taken under Constance Crane's wing when she first came to Mill Hall to work. That gentlewoman had shown a personal interest in the girl, even giving her extra lessons in spinning and candle making.

"Can such a good person be a witch?" Jennet wondered aloud. Though she herself still harbored doubts about Mistress Crane—the woman had been one of Sir Robert's mistresses, after all—Jennet could tell that Emma worshiped her.

"Certes, she never done what they say!" The moment the words were out, Emma slapped both hands over her mouth. Above them, her eyes were wide and terrified.

"What do you fear, Emma? Faith, I do not intend to betray your confidences." Without batting an eyelid, Jennet told yet another lie. "In truth, I share your high opinion of the gentlewoman."

Relief made Emma weep. In between great gulping sobs, the rest of her story tumbled out. All the Mill Hall servants had liked Mistress Crane's way of running the household and liked her, as well. It had only been after her arrest that some of them had begun to insist she was evil, that she'd sinned with Peter Marsh, that she'd killed him.

"What the cook said—I do not think even he believes it be true. But 'tis what everyone says now." Emma sniffled and wiped her eyes with the backs of her hands, reminding Jennet of the way her own children wept.

According to Emma, the servants now vied with each other to remember and reinterpret past events. A death after using one of Lucy Milborne's herbal remedies. Constance Crane in earnest conversation with Peter Marsh during the time he lived at Mill Hall.

"What can you tell me about Peter Marsh?" Jennet asked.

But Emma had scarce known him. He kept to himself.

"You must have heard something about him."

Even after several minutes of careful consideration, Emma had little more to offer. Only that Master Marsh had lived at Mill Hall for two or three years and that no one knew why he'd left.

"But he went at about the time the chaplain came?"

"Aye." Emma's face scrunched with the effort of remembering. "Sir Adrian came for to see Master Garrard, and the next thing we knew, Master Marsh had tooken hissel off."

Jennet lowered her voice and placed one hand on the handle of Emma's basket. "Might Peter Marsh have fled because he was a secret Papist?"

Emma's eyes widened. She shook her head in fearful denial.

Jennet wondered if she had stumbled onto a clue. If Marsh had been breaking the laws on religion, he might have feared Sir Adrian Ridley would find him out, though how his faith could have led to Marsh's murder, Jennet had no notion.

"Now, Emma," she began, but her line of questioning had frightened the girl.

"Give it me," Emma pleaded, pulling at her basket. "I durn't say more."

When Jennet released her hold on the handle, the contents almost tipped out in the servant maid's haste to escape.

"Wait. Please. One more question. I have heard that Mistress Crane kept a familiar. A cat."

So vigorously did Emma shake her head that her cap came loose. "She never done that. She ain't able to abide the creatures. She does sneeze hersel boss-eyed whenever that old she cat that lives in the stable comes near."

That said, Emma hurried away. Jennet did not trouble to follow her. Instead she wandered deeper into Mill Hall's gardens, coming at length to a small knot garden. At the far side, a single gardener toiled.

Finding a convenient bench, Jennet sat to mull over what she had learned. Her head soon began to ache. Faith, she had more questions now than when she'd left Lady Appleton sleeping. A new idea or two was all very well, but she'd hoped to be able to present her mistress with a few answers, too.

At first, Jennet did not pay the gardener much mind. It was only after she realized that he was of an age with Lucy Milborne that she took an interest in him.

Hoisting herself up off the bench, Jennet smoothed her skirts, moistened her lips, and fixed her most engaging smile firmly in place.

19

Susanna awoke with a drowsy head and a sense of confusion. For a moment, she did not know where she was or why she felt so lethargic. Then she remembered the sleeping draught she'd taken to counteract the painful stinging in her hand.

Aware of the potential after-effects, she'd debated with herself before swallowing a dose of poppy syrup. She'd decided that Jennet, who had already gone off to find out what she could from the Mill Hall servants, had the right of it. She required rest in order to recover. Now she wondered if she'd made a mistake. She also needed to have her wits about her at supper if she was to discover a way to help Constance and Lucy.

"But we are to sup here in this chamber," Jennet announced when Susanna sat up and stated her intention. "I am to send for a servant when you feel hungry."

"Send now." Susanna swung her legs over the side of the bed and waited impatiently for the room to stop spinning. "Why are we quarantined?"

"We keep to this chamber because Master Garrard keeps to his."

"Ah."

When their evening repast had been delivered, Susanna descended from the high bedstead, with Jennet's help, and wrapped herself in the soft velvet folds of a loose-bodied gown. Her mind, at least, had once more begun to function with its usual efficiency.

"What have you been able to find out while I slept?"

Surprised at how hungry she was, she accepted the first course and maneuvered the spoon to her mouth with care. Her movements were made awkward by the tenderness of her hand, but she savored the spicy goodness of a beef broth while Jennet repeated her conversations with the cook and with a maidservant named Emma.

When she'd also polished off a caudle, Susanna looked hopefully for more solid fare. "There is an alarming pattern in what both of us have been told. Someone seems to have gone to a great deal of trouble to place blame on Lucy and Constance. Most of the stories being told about them were copied direct from that pamphlet about the witchcraft trials in Chelmsford."

"I recognized the similarities, too." Jennet brought a covered dish to the small table at which Susanna sat to eat. "And yet it may be that all witches behave the same way. I am not convinced Mistress Milborne is innocent."

"You believe Mildred Edgecumbe? You think there are marks all over Lucy's body where a cat, or a toad, or mayhap a dog, did suckle blood?"

"I saw no marks such as the ones Mistress Edgecumbe described, but Lucy Milborne is trough-eyed."

Susanna helped herself to a portion of pigeon pie. It had been well cooked in minced parsley and onions with ground garlic and vinegar. "I did not notice any such deformity." But she'd seen the woman only once, in gaol. The light had been poor, and for the most part Lucy had kept her head bowed, hiding not just her eyes but her entire face.

"She looks like a witch."

Susanna did not bother to reprimand Jennet. People feared what they did not understand, and there were many things that had no explanation. It was even possible there were witches, or at least individuals who had skills or senses most people lacked. But Susanna was certain of one thing—Clement Edgecumbe and Peter Marsh had not died of a witch's curse.

"You say that the charge that Constance kept a cat, her familiar, was a fabrication?"

"Aye."

"When any lie is repeated often enough, there are those who will come to believe it was the truth all along."

Susanna took a bite of sallet, appreciative of the tasty blend of parsley, sage, garlic, onions, leeks, borage, mint, fennel, cresses, rue, rosemary, and purslane, all mingled with oil, vinegar, and salt. The ale the cook had sent with the meal was excellent, too—well brewed, properly aged, and smelling faintly of germander. All in all, this meal was a far cry from the previous night's fare. Either the cook did not like preparing fish, or the poor quality of that food had been meant to discourage them from staying on at Mill Hall.

"I grow fanciful," she murmured. And she was remarkably tired for someone who had slept all afternoon. She had a suspicion that she might have taken too much of the sleeping draught.

"What will you do next?" Jennet's question jerked Susanna's attention back to the matter at hand.

"We need to compile a list of suspects."

Jennet produced paper and Susanna's own penner and cleared away the remains of the meal, but when Susanna took up the quill, she winced. "You will have to inscribe the names," she told Jennet.

"You are in pain."

"A little."

"I am out of practice," Jennet warned. "I was taught to write as well as to read years ago, at the command of your father, but I've had little use for the writing. It is rare I am called upon to do so much as sign my own name."

"Print large, then, and the names will be legible enough. Start with Hugo Garrard."

As Jennet complied, Susanna explained her reasoning. "His grudging manner, curt speech, even all that ostentatious praying are not suspicious in themselves, but it is curious that he was so reluctant to talk with me. As head of the family, should he not be open to any suggestion that Lucy and Constance are innocent?"

"Unless he killed Peter Marsh and would use his cousins as scapegoats."

"Why kill Marsh?"

That Jennet had a theory did not surprise Susanna, nor did its farfetched nature.

"A Papist? Marsh? But that would only be more likely to provide a motive for Marsh to kill Sir Adrian Ridley."

"What if Marsh was about to betray Mistress Milborne to the new chaplain? She bewitched him to save herself. You were right about her having been a nun. She was in a convent near Canterbury. When it was dissolved, she came back here to her childhood home, but instead of living at Mill Hall, she moved into that cottage. A gardener remembered it," she explained.

Jennet's smug expression told Susanna she'd been saving these revelations in the hope of making an impression.

"Good work, Jennet." The praise was sincere, but so were Susanna's reservations. "And yet, having once been a nun is not against the law. And the penalty for failing to attend church is naught but a fine."

"There might have been more serious punishments if she had harbored a Roman Catholic priest and heard mass. What if Marsh intended to claim that was the case?"

Would Lucy have killed to stop him? It would have been his word against hers and she was a gentlewoman. To Susanna's mind, murder seemed an extreme reaction.

"What reason would Lucy have had to harm Edgecumbe?" she asked. "What threat did he pose? The two deaths are linked. Of that I feel certain."

"They both died by witchcraft." Unable to think of a better answer, Jennet frowned and drew squiggly lines on the paper.

"They both died of poison," Susanna corrected her. "Or so I believe. When I've talked to that stableboy, and to Damascin Edgecumbe, I hope to confirm my suspicion that banewort killed them."

"Banewort?"

"Aye. Huge bushes grew near the wych elm. Did you not notice them? The ones with the large black berries. They contain a most deadly poison."

"But when those men died, there would not yet have been any berries."

"The leaves are as fatal as the fruit. Write the name Mildred Edgecumbe beneath Hugo's. The widow is always a suspect when her husband dies of a sudden." Susanna had reason to be well aware of that fact. "Underneath, put down Damascin, for she found Marsh's body. Indeed, she is the only one, at present, with a clear connection to both victims."

Jennet obliged, hesitating over the spelling of Damascin. Then, on her own initiative, she added Lucy Milborne's name.

"Is it not possible that Mistress Milborne is guilty even if Mistress Crane is not? Mistress Edgecumbe never once mentioned Mistress Crane."

"True enough."

As she mulled that over, Susanna stared through the window at the spire of the chapel they'd passed en route to Lucy's cottage. The sun was about to set, reminding her that she'd slept half the day away.

"Why would Lucy kill two men? And do not tell me she is a witch and needs no reason but to do evil. Give another reason."

"The gardener said she kept to herself. He called her an anchor."

After a moment's thought, Susanna made sense of this. "Anchoress?"

"That was it."

"The term means no more than a sort of religious hermit."

Susanna frowned. Memories were long and anti-Catholic feeling strong in this part of Kent. Was that all that was behind the accusations against Lucy? Hatred of Papists?

"We must delve more deeply into Lucy's past," she said. "Find out if she had some connection to Clement Edgecumbe other than being neighbors. How did the Edgecumbes acquire their land? If it was confiscated from the Catholic Church, that might be reason for Lucy to resent them."

"A motive for murder?"

"Lucy could have killed one or both men. I admit it." But she did not think it likely.

Emboldened, Jennet added Constance Crane's name to the list. "She could be lying about Marsh and what he was to her. The servants here saw them together. Close together." Unspoken was the reminder that Constance had been Robert's mistress, reason enough for Jennet's poor opinion of her character.

Susanna took the list from her and studied it. "Let us consider first why someone else might have wanted to make Lucy and Constance seem guilty. Most, perhaps all of what is being said about them was first bandied about only after Marsh's death. Otherwise charges against Lucy would have been made much sooner. The clever planting of rumors following their arrest did as much harm as anything that came before. Someone read that pamphlet and copied its contents."

Who would want both Edgecumbe and Marsh dead? Who would want one of them dead? Who would profit from Lucy's death? From Constance's? Susanna knew there must be connections between the two murders, and between Lucy and Constance and the deaths, and between Lucy and Constance and those who could have arranged matters so that they would be blamed. All she had to do was find them.

"If Edgecumbe's wife and daughter believed Mistress Milborne caused his death, could they have plotted to implicate her in Marsh's death in order to punish her?"

"An interesting theory, Jennet, but it does not explain why Marsh was murdered. Or why Constance should also be blamed. Or even how or why Master Edgecumbe died."

"What about that fellow Norden?"

Susanna brightened. "Yes. I had almost forgotten him. How far is he prepared to go to get material for that pamphlet he is writing?" She handed the paper back. "Add his name to the list."

"Then there is Arthur Kennison." Jennet wrote him down, too.

"Was he Garrard's messenger to Edgecumbe Manor,

as seems likely? And if he was, what messages did he carry?"

Crestfallen, Jennet admitted she had not asked. "Estate matters?"

"Perhaps. We must inquire further."

"Anyone else?" Jennet held the quill poised above the paper.

"Add one more. Write down Sir Adrian Ridley."

"The preacher?"

"Why not?" She yawned and moved toward the bed.

Perhaps she was growing fanciful herself, Susanna thought. Certes, in spite of all the sleep she'd gotten, she was already too tired to think straight.

"If we must consider everyone, why not Sir Adrian? He might have killed in order to further his own career. Suppose Constance confessed to him that she was possessed by the devil. Would he not gain considerable renown among those who were in exile with him? Many of them came back to England convinced that the spread of witchcraft was imminent."

Unable to focus on the puzzle any longer, Susanna crawled beneath the covers. "We will discuss this further in the morning," she mumbled, and in the next instant surrendered to exhaustion.

20

Lady Appleton, and therefore Jennet, rose early on the second morning at Mill Hall. Jennet had hoped they'd stay longer, that the burnt hand would have more time to heal and so that she, Jennet, could continue to make inroads with Master Garrard's servants. For that reason, she had added two lettuce cakes to Lady Appleton's food. Her mistress carried these thin brown wafers, made from the white juice of wild lettuce, as a sleeping aid. One was the usual dose.

They'd worked well. Too well. Jennet had not expected them to take effect so rapidly or cause such deep sleep. She'd spent the night pacing the bedchamber, keeping watch over the woman she'd drugged, afraid she'd dispensed too much of the medication.

It appeared she had not. Lady Appleton seemed as alert and vigorous as ever. At first light, she dispatched Lionel to Canterbury with a message addressed to Martin Calthorpe, a scholar of some renown and a friend of Lady Appleton's late father. Soon after, Jennet was riding apillion behind Fulke as they set out on horseback for Edgecumbe Manor.

There they learned that Mistress Damascin and her mother had also been up betimes. They'd left for Maidstone before dawn.

Deprived of any immediate opportunity to speak with the young woman who'd found Marsh's body, Lady Appleton asked instead for Edmund, the stable-boy who'd come upon Master Edgecumbe when he lay dying.

She had no authority to question him, nor any excuse to go into Edgecumbe Manor's stables, but she was not above taking advantage of a household in an uproar following the precipitous departure of its mistress.

"Look after the horses, Fulke," she ordered. "And you, Jennet, see what you can learn from the other servants."

Soon Jennet was comfortably ensconced in the kitchen. Yawning as she sipped a restorative cup of ale, she grumbled companionably about the lack of consideration of employers. This created an immediate bond. It did not take long for her to discover that the servants had much more liking for Clement Edgecumbe than for either his wife or his daughter.

"Mistress Edgecumbe has a temper."

"And a sharp tongue."

"And hard hands," said the dairy maid, reaching up to rub one ear.

"Did she scold her husband, too?" Jennet asked.

"He knew how to keep her in her place, that old man."

"How old?"

No one seemed to know precisely, but they all agreed Master Edgecumbe had been much older than his wife. Older, even, than Lucy Milborne. And, as Lady Appleton had suspected, although he came from the area, he had not acquired this property until the dissolution of the monasteries. Like so many others of the New Religion, he'd benefited from the confiscation of Church property by the Crown.

"Did he know Lucy Milborne before she was a nun?" Jennet asked.

"Might have," the dairy maid told her. "They did quarrel like two old friends."

"How did he get along with the rest of his neighbors?"

"None had aught to complain of."

"I heard talk of marriage," the cook put in. "Between Mistress Damascin and Hugo Garrard. Till Master Edgecumbe changed his mind."

"Or Mistress Damascin did. She could do better, pretty as she is." This from a plain-faced maidservant.

"And vain about it, too." The dairy maid, whose complexion was appropriately milk white, seemed to think herself passing attractive.

"She's generous with what she has, is Mistress Damascin."

"When did she ever share anything that was hers?"

"Margery gets all her cast off clothes, and some of them are scarce worn." Envy laced the words.

"Who is Margery?" Jennet asked the maidservant.

"Mistress Damascin's tiring maid. She got to go to Maidstone, too."

Jennet resolved to make the acquaintance of this Margery.

21

I would hear, in your own words, what befell your master" Susanna said to the stableboy. He was a thin lad, still growling, and he had yet to develop much in the way of muscles. A few preliminary questions had established that he'd been employed at Edgecumbe Manor for only a few months.

"I know nothing, madam. I had naught to do with it."

"You found him, here in the stable, or so I am told."

A reluctant nod answered her.

"Was he already unconscious?"

That question earned her a negative shake of the head.

Gentling her voice, Susanna urged young Edmund to describe the symptoms he had observed. She was not surprised by what he revealed. Clement Edgecumbe had been wildeyed, incapable of speech. As the servant had watched in horror, the master had fallen and been unable to rise. At that point, Edmund had at last run for help. By the time he'd returned, accompanied by Mildred and several other people, Edgecumbe had been deeply unconscious. He had never afterward regained his senses.

All this could have been caused by ingesting banewort.

"Did Master Edgecumbe arrive at this stable after you were already here? Or was he here before you entered?"

"He was here when I comed in to feed the beasts."

"Do you have any idea where he had been?" At his blank look, she clarified her question. "Was he dressed for indoors or out? For riding, mayhap?"

But the boy was no help to her. If he'd noticed, he could no longer remember. "He was a good master," he mumbled. "The old master was a good man."

"And your mistress? Is she a good woman?"

Edmund would speak no ill of Mildred Edgecumbe and had only praise for Damascin. "She said I deserved a reward for trying to help her father. A week agone, she gave me an entire new suit of clothes and took away the old one I growed out of."

Susanna suspected the garments would be counted as part of the boy's yearly wages, but chose not to disillusion him. It was plain he adored pretty Mistress Damascin. Likely all the menservants here felt much the same.

When Susanna determined that she could learn nothing more from young Edmund, she thanked him with a new-minted penny and left the stable. Soon after, she departed Edgecumbe Manor.

Once Susanna, Jennet, and Fulke were on their way again, she asked Jennet for an account of everything she'd learned. The telling took some time.

"Hugo was courting Damascin?" Susanna exclaimed in surprise. No one at Mill Hall had so much as hinted that such a match might be in the offing. "I wonder if that is why Kennison was on his way to Edgecumbe Manor that morning."

"If Mistress Damascin became Mistress Garrard, that might have left Mistress Crane without a home." Jennet advanced her latest theory with as much eagerness as she'd suggested earlier ones. "A younger woman might resent having an elder about and send her packing."

"But why would that be cause for Constance to kill Clement Edgecumbe, especially if Clement did not plan to give his approval to the marriage?"

Jennet's reasoning did not account for Marsh's death, either.

Had Clement stood in the way of the wedding? Susanna was not convinced of it. It seemed more logical that Damascin would have objected to the match. Such a pretty young woman might be expected to set her cap higher, angling for a knight, perhaps. And yet, in all practical ways, the union would be an excellent one. Both parties were gently born. Hugo was six or seven years Damascin's senior. More importantly, the marriage would combine Mill Hall and Edgecumbe Manor lands into one large and prosperous estate. Any father ought to be pleased by such an arrangement.

But what if Clement Edgecumbe *had* changed his mind? Susanna considered this possibility and its ramifications as they continued on toward Canterbury. If he had objected to the match after favoring it, something must have prompted the change of heart.

Had that something also been the reason he'd been murdered?

22

Stone Street, the old Roman road from Aldington to Canterbury, was straight and paved but not as well maintained as Jennet had hoped. It was overgrown with trees and bushes and in places was well-nigh impassable. Worse, by the time they'd entered the twelve-mile stretch she'd contemplated with such longing on the way south, it was already well past noon. They had to ride hard the rest of the day in order to reach their destination by nightfall.

The pace might have been bearable if it had meant going home to Leigh Abbey on the morrow. Instead they would be returning to Maidstone. Lady Appleton had intended to go there all along, and now that Mistress Edgecumbe and her daughter were already en route, she would make even greater haste to get there.

Jennet was ready to fall from her pillion by the time they arrived in Canterbury, too exhausted to admire the majesty of the cathedral or take particular notice of any less dominant surroundings. All that mattered was that Master Martin Calthorpe welcomed their small party into his house and made them comfortable with food, drink, and soft, cushioned places to sit.

Indeed, Master Calthorpe showed a flattering eagerness to be of service, even after Lady Appleton explained that she'd come to him in search of information about a convent. This announcement momentarily took him aback.

"St. Sepulchre's? Why, that's been gone since the Dissolution." He stroked his long silver beard and looked bemused.

"But you remember it. Someone in Canterbury must know more. Something about the nuns who lived there."

"Only the most notorious." At Lady Appleton's questioning look he chuckled. "The Nun of Kent was at St. Sepulchre's for a short time. Before she was burnt to death for treason."

Lady Appleton frowned. "The Nun of Kent?" she inquired.

"You would have been a baby at the time. 'Tis no wonder you do not remember. Her real name was Barton. Elizabeth Barton."

At the surname, Jennet looked up, startled, for she had been born a Barton herself.

"She had visions. Made prophecies. For several years she was lauded as a holy woman. She lived near the archbishop's palace at Aldington and so came to his attention. She was brought here and put in the Benedictine priory of St. Sepulchre's and called a nun, though I do not believe she ever took holy orders."

"When I was a child," Lady Appleton murmured, "just before King Henry closed all the nunneries and monasteries."

Master Calthorpe nodded. "She spoke out against the king's divorce. That was why she was executed. For treason."

"She would have been at the convent when Lucy Milborne was a nun there. And Lucy Milborne lived near Aldington before she was a nun."

And after, Jennet thought. Did any of this have significance? The dissolution of the monasteries had been complete well before she'd been old enough to care about matters more immediate than her next meal or a new poppet to play with. The only time in Jennet's memory when Catholicism had been openly practiced in England had been during the brief reign of Queen Mary and even then, at Leigh Abbey, their household had continued to observe the tenets of the New Religion.

"How can I trace a woman who was a nun in this convent?" Lady Appleton asked.

"There are few documents left from that time. Indeed, had it not been for certain churchmen with a desire to increase their own libraries, all the contents of the religious houses would have been destroyed."

"They saved books?" Lady Appleton looked hopeful. "Where there are books, there might also be papers. Records."

Her injury, which had been too tender to hide inside a glove, caught Master Calthorpe's attention as she touched her fingers to his arm. At once he made a fuss over her, which seemed to pain her as much as the hand did, and it was some time before they returned to the subject that most concerned her.

"There may have been something written down back then," she explained when she had given him a brief account of the events she was investigating, "that will explain why someone would falsely accuse Lucy Milborne of being a witch."

But Master Calthorpe shook his head. With nervous fingers, he twisted one strand of his beard. "The books, many of them old and valuable, and most of them dealing with religious subjects in Latin or Greek, were deemed worthy of preservation. But all else the Papists had was destroyed. Even the tomb of Thomas Becket here in Canterbury was torn apart. In the year of our Lord fifteen hundred and thirty-eight, it was.

The monastery at Canterbury was dissolved two years later."

Leigh Abbey had been church land once, Jennet remembered. Lady Appleton's grandfather had received it as a reward for service to King Henry and erected his fine great house where the abbey had once stood. He'd probably torn down the old building and used its stones in the new. That was what most builders did.

"Over four hundred relics used to be kept in Canterbury," Calthorpe continued. "It was a destination for thousands of pilgrims. All gone now." He sighed. "You must not think I miss the old religion, but Canterbury's prosperity has declined without shrines to visit. No one comes here anymore."

"There must be someone who remembers the nuns at St. Sepulchre."

"It was suppressed over thirty years ago. Dame Philippa John was the last prioress, but she died in the same year as King Henry."

"Lucy Milborne is alive. There may be others."

Master Calthorpe shook his head over the hopelessness of Lady Appleton's quest and reminded her that she might be wrong about the accused witches, but he assured her he would do all he could to find any convent records.

The next morning, Lady Appleton's party set out for Maidstone.

"I will make further inquiries and send on whatever I discover," Master Calthorpe promised, "but have a care in the interim."

"Does he think you are in danger?" Jennet asked as they rode north.

"He believes Lucy Milborne may indeed be a witch and that I risk contagion by helping her."

Jennet saw that this troubled her mistress, but she

also knew that Master Calthorpe's warnings would do no more to persuade her to desist than Jennet's had.

Their route took them past the former convent, a quarter mile from the city walls and almost adjacent to Watling Street. As far as Jennet could see, there was little left in the buildings to suggest a nunnery.

A little later, after Watling Street had veered northwest toward Faversham, Lady Appleton lifted her hand, now covered with a soft and supple leather glove, to point toward the east. "That way lies the Forest of Blean. Master Calthorpe told me that the nuns used to gather fuel there, in an area called Minchen Wood."

Jennet's ears perked up. "What else did they do there?"

"What do you suppose?" Lady Appleton asked.

Jennet lowered her voice. "Pagan rites? Witchcraft?"

"You confuse your religions, Jennet. Next you will tell me that Mildred and Damascin are witches, too. That they place blame on Lucy and Constance to hide their own evil doings."

In the face of Lady Appleton's gentle mockery, Jennet said no more. The thought *had* crossed her mind and she could not entirely dismiss it.

They traveled on, endlessly, it seemed to Jennet. For long stretches they saw no sign of life, unless one counted an occasional red squirrel or a fox. Once, Lady Appleton stopped to admire a field of lavender, but for the most part she kept up the same killing pace she'd set the day before. She was anxious now to get back to Maidstone and find out what Master Baldwin had discovered.

Jennet was of two minds about Master Baldwin. She remained concerned that a liaison between her mistress and the London man was a mistake. On the other hand, he might be the only person left with enough influence over Lady Appleton to persuade that gentle-

woman to abandon her championship of Constance
Crane and Lucy Milborne.

They'd all be gathered in Maidstone for the Assizes,
Jennet realized. All those who would give testimony
against the witches. All those Lady Appleton suspected
of killing Master Edgecumbe and Master Marsh by poison. And Lady Appleton, in her quest for justice,
meant to delve into their private lives and confront
them with whatever secrets she uncovered.

Such meddling could only lead to trouble.

Still, Jennet was glad to see the rooftops of Maidstone when they appeared up ahead. She remembered
the comfortable accommodations at Master Baldwin's
house and decided she would indulge herself and take
advantage of the water left in the hot bath Lady Appleton was sure to ask for. She'd discovered a leather
tub during their last stay.

With a little sigh of anticipation, Jennet imagined
herself sitting in it before the fire, surrounded by
steaming, scented water. She inhaled deeply, but the
only smell that reached her was that of fish. While
she'd been daydreaming, they'd entered the town.
They were riding through the marketplace.

"Lady Appleton!" a man called from the corn cross
at the top of the High Street, where those engaged in
the grain trade gathered. It was Master Baldwin's servant, Simon. "I've been waiting here to head off your
party before you reached the house." He doffed his
hat and handed over the note he'd been keeping inside it.

Dismay suffused her features as Lady Appleton read
the short message. "It seems we will be staying at an
inn for the rest of our sojourn in Maidstone."

"What has happened?"

"Why, Jennet," Lady Appleton teased her. "I
thought you would be pleased. 'Tis much more re-

spectable for me to stay at the Queen's Arms while Nick remains in his own house."

"But why, madam? What possible reason could he have for turning you out?" To her own surprise, Jennet felt offended at the snub.

"The best of reasons. He has another guest, one who would prefer, I do think, to avoid my company."

"Another woman?"

"Aye." Lady Appleton was smiling, but Jennet did not see the joke.

"What woman?"

"The only one who has a right to dictate to him," Lady Appleton said. "His mother."

23

In Maidstone, cloth was sold at the schoolhouse. Winifred Baldwin did not spend long examining the offerings. She was convinced Nick had wanted her out of the house for some reason, and that did not sit well with her. Besides, she felt it her patriotic duty to disdain these so-called new draperies.

"Cursed foreigners," she muttered, glaring at the assortment of grograms, mockados, and sackcloth produced by Maidstone's newly acquired community of Dutch cloth workers, men and their families who'd fled the oppression of Catholic overlords in the Low Countries. "What was wrong with good English broadcloth, I'd like to know!" Nose in the air, she gave a disdainful sniff and went on her way.

Once, men of Kent had made naught but broadcloth and a few of the short cloths called manikins. Now everyone seemed bent on variety.

Winifred was already in ill humor when her route took her past the Queen's Arms. She stopped dead in her tracks at what she saw there. Toby, the servant Nick had sent with her to carry her purchases, almost ran into her, but she scarce noticed.

That woman was just dismounting from one of those newfangled sidesaddles in front of the inn.

"What is she doing here?" Winifred muttered.

"Lady Appleton came for the Assizes," Toby said.

She turned to glare at him. "And how do you know that?"

"That was what Master Baldwin told the cook."

"And why should he tell the cook anything about Lady Appleton?"

"Because she was his guest here just a few days ago, madam."

"What?" Winifred's voice rose in tandem with her agitation.

Realizing at last that he'd said more than he should have, the lad turned beet red and attempted to recant his statements. Winifred would have none of it. She seized him by the earlobe to bring his face close to her own.

"Tell me everything you know, you poxy knave, or I will carve your heart out and eat it for supper."

24

"What happened?" Before Susanna could hide the damage, Nick seized her wrist to lift and examine her hand by the flickering flame of the nearest candle. They were in her chamber at the Queen's Arms, alone for the nonce. A few minutes before Nick's arrival, Jennet, Fulke, and Lionel had descended to the common room below to search out some supper.

Making light of her injury, Susanna allowed him to cradle her hand while she gave him an edited version of the mishap at Edgecumbe Manor. When she stopped speaking, Nick scowled first at her and then at the ugly, peeling skin.

"Are you certain it was an accident? Remember what happened to you in London two years ago. You got too close to the truth for someone's comfort and were attacked."

"I remember." It had been thanks to Nick she'd survived. And he'd only known to come to her rescue because Winifred Baldwin had caught sight of the man following Susanna. She'd told her son. Susanna shot him a cheeky grin. "I wonder—do you suppose your mother ever regrets having given the warning that saved me?"

"This is not a matter for levity, Susanna." Nick glowered at her. "You've set yourself a thankless task. Put yourself in danger."

She dismissed his worries with a careless flick of her uninjured hand and crossed the room to a window seat. "Come and sit down beside me, Nick. I have more to tell you. The most important thing is that I believe the charges against Lucy and Constance were copied from a pamphlet written about the witch trials last year in Chelmsford."

"A pamphlet?" His brow still furrowed, he was unable to hide his concern, but neither was he able to resist her invitation. He joined her at the window, bracing one hand against the wall, one foot at the base of the bench, as if he would make of himself her protective shield.

"Yes. A pamphlet. You know the sort. Badly illustrated with woodcuts. The likeness purported to be Mother Waterhouse could have been any woman in a kirtle and an old-fashioned gable headdress. The facial features, in particular, were indistinct."

In spite of his worry for her, his lips twitched. "How did you come to notice the similarities? Cheap print is not your usual reading matter."

She smiled back. "No. Although I must admit that I went on to read the entire account once I'd opened the pamphlet and begun. I came by it when a chapman carried copies into Kent and Jennet bought one. Indeed, I still might not have known anything of it if Rosamond had not, on one particular day in late April, suffered an upset stomach from eating too many sweets."

At Nick's look of confusion, Susanna smiled again, but now the expression was bittersweet. She had not realized until this moment just how much she missed the pleasant domesticity of Leigh Abbey. And Rosamond, too, certes.

"When Rosamond came to live with me, Jennet offered to relieve me of the daily reading to the maidservants. I put no restrictions on her selections, thinking it unnecessary."

Bewildered, Nick stared at her. "You read to your maids?"

"Reading aloud to the servants is a ritual my grandmother taught me to observe when I was very young. In this way a gentlewoman can improve the minds of her retainers and at the same time give painless instruction. Grandmother favored manuals on various aspects of household management and stodgy religious treatises translated from Latin. She would have been shocked at Jennet's choice of reading material."

She had been passing the open door to the small parlor, Susanna remembered, when her attention had been caught by a few ominous words: "And also that he should kill a man, and so he did."

Instead of continuing on to her stillroom, she'd quietly entered the room. Jennet had been sitting by the window, a book on her lap and a cluster of maidservants at her feet.

"I was reluctant to interfere," she told Nick when she'd described the scene to him. "The pamphlet, titled *The Examination and confession of certain Witches at Chelmsford in the County of Essex,* could scarce improve anyone's mind, but neither did it seem likely to do harm."

"I should think it would frighten impressionable young servants."

"They enjoy being afraid. As Jennet continued to read, something about a cat turning itself into a toad, Grace and Hester, the two new girls I am training, shivered and clung to each other in an ecstasy of delighted fright. Doll the dairy maid, Joyce the laundress, and Martha the maid of all work, were less demonstrative but seemed equally engrossed in the story. None of them noticed I had joined them until I spoke."

She paused in her story to wonder how Hester was managing. Susanna had hoped the young woman, tall and rawboned and still growing into her body, would make a good nursery maid, but she'd shown little enthusiasm in her dealings with Rosamond.

"Go on," Nick prompted, putting an end to Susanna's woolgathering.

"Jennet defended her choice by claiming the reading material was a cautionary tale. She pointed out that the maids could not guard themselves against evil unless they were taught how to recognize it. Then she turned my own words against me to remind me that I have often said that all knowledge is good."

"How did you deal with that argument?"

"I did not have to. Lavinia took care of the matter."

For a moment, he looked blank. "The cat?"

"Yes." Lavinia was a long-haired white feline, a descendant of the remarkable Bala, a cat Nick had brought back with him from Persia. "She chose that moment to streak across the room. Grace screamed in fright. Joyce threw her apron over her head. I was hard put not to laugh, but I made my voice and my expression as stern as I could and told them they had naught to fear from cat or toad. Indeed, I pointed out that the cats at Leigh Abbey do only good and that we would soon be overrun with mice and other vermin if not for their vigilance. Then I sent them back to their duties and suggested Jennet find another book to read on the morrow. She was most put out with me."

"You are too easy on her. She gets ideas above her station."

"Jennet is my friend as well as my housekeeper," Susanna reminded him. "And I can scarce blame her for her choice when I had myself already broadened the curriculum to include a sprinkling of almanacs, herbals, and tales of chivalry. I should have realized that Jennet, unsupervised, would be drawn to even more popular works, the sort that appeal to her avid interest in anything scandalous."

"You did not, I perceive, convince any of them, not even Jennet, that they had naught to fear from witches."

"No. There are some things a master cannot command from a servant. It seemed more productive to make sure I had an adequate supply of blessed thistle." At his questioning look, she clarified, amused for some perverse reason by the sudden hint of alarm in his eyes. "It is thought to ward off evil when pinned to one's clothing." She shrugged. "I also ground a small portion of galingale to powder, in case anyone asked for some. Many people believe that burning it can break a spell or ward off a curse.

"For God's sake, Susanna! Do not speak of such things."

"Nick, you worry too much."

His expression turned thunderous. "And you, beloved, do not worry enough."

25

Constance and Lucy might have been accused of crimes against God and State, but that did not excuse them from attending church services. On the Sunday before the Assizes were scheduled to begin, they were hustled out of their cell and into the interrogation room, along with the rest of the poor unfortunates awaiting trial.

Two other women charged as witches were there. Their names had been flung at Constance during one of her interrogations, as if she should know them both. Agnes Bennett of Boughton Monchelsea was a widow. She had been accused of being incited by the instigation of the devil to use enchantments and potions to destroy a child, a boy who had died instantly upon being bewitched. Or so they said. And so Agnes herself said, now. After months of imprisonment and countless questionings, she had become convinced that she was a witch.

"Confess," she urged Constance with a high, hysterical cackle. "They will feed you well if you do."

"The food you speak of came from a generous gentlewoman." That same gentlewoman had paid the fee to exempt Constance and Lucy from being chained to the wall like animals.

But Agnes was beyond listening to reason. "Confess. Confess. And be saved."

"Confess and die," Lucy muttered.

The other woman accused of witchcraft was named Cecilia West, a spinster, but the charge against her was not bewitching to death. Her victim, the daughter of one William Loppam of Bethersden, was not dead. She had despaired of her life after being bewitched, but had recovered. Celia would be sentenced, at worst, to a year's imprisonment. She had already discovered the way to survive it. She agreed with everything anyone asked of her, save only that she was in league with other witches or the devil, and stayed silent the remainder of the time.

When all the prisoners had been assembled, Adrian Ridley conducted services, railing against witchcraft in his sermon. It occurred to Constance as she listened to him that the difference between charms and prayers was very slight. Both used Latin phrases similar to those in the liturgy, incorporated holy names, and based their effectiveness on the power of God.

Even the bedtime prayer taught to children could be interpreted as a night spell. "Matthew, Mark, Luke, and John," she murmured, "bless the bed that I lie on."

A little later, back in their cell, she shared her insight with Lucy. Her cousin had been much more cheerful since Lady Appleton's food baskets started arriving. She chuckled to herself at Constance's comment.

"What amuses you?"

"That you still think common sense can save us. 'Tis not whether or not I am a witch that condemns me. Know that. 'Tis my adherence to my faith."

"Then convince them you have given up your faith. It is not as if you have refused to attend church all these years." Lucy had always given the appearance of conforming, until charges of witchcraft had been made against her. Since then, she'd seemed to take unmitigated delight in reminding people she had once been a nun. She'd crossed herself at least a dozen times during today's services.

"The Catholic Church sanctions the use of written charms. There is no wickedness in attaching holy words about a person's neck, provided they contain nothing false or suspect. Have you never heard of Pope Leo's amulet? 'Tis worn against harm in battle and relies upon the repetition of the names of God and three paternosters."

"What I have heard is that using the name of Jesus to drive away the devil or prevent witchcraft is condemned because ignorant people might come to think of Christ as a conjurer." Constance's voice was sharp with irritation.

Lucy warmed to the argument. "Do you discount the effect of all charms, then? Is it more foolish to wear a cross and make the sign of it than to tie a bit of rowan inside your clothes with red thread to ward off evil? Your friend Sir Adrian would have it that any combination of herbs is magic and to be avoided, but I warrant you he'd accept a healing potion quick enough if he thought he was dying."

"He is not my friend."

Lucy snorted and said no more, leaving Constance to brood in silence. Her thoughts remained on Adrian, on his betrayal. She'd believed she could trust him. She'd even thought, briefly, that he admired her as a man admires a woman.

The creaking of the door announced they had a visitor. She expected to see the man she'd been thinking of, as if thinking of him could conjure him up. Adrian Ridley *had* come at least once a day to visit them. To torment Constance.

Instead, Susanna Appleton entered the cell.

Constance stared at her with an odd mixture of gratitude and resentment. Given their encounter after Sir Robert Appleton's death, it was remarkable that his widow had decided to come to Constance's assistance, even belatedly. That she now seemed determined to help her husband's former mistress of a sudden struck Constance as peculiar. She knew she would be passing foolish to refuse any offer of assistance, no matter the source, but she could not quite dismiss her uneasiness. Did this woman, like Adrian Ridley, have ulterior motives for involving herself in the case?

"Are you well?" Lady Appleton inquired.

"As you can see, we received your generous gifts." The water to bathe in had been surpassing welcome.

"No thanks are necessary."

Another woman, the same female who had accompanied Lady Appleton on her last visit, bustled into the room behind her mistress. She carried a capcase, one Constance recognized. The small traveling bag was her own.

"You did go to Mill Hall."

"I sent word to you that such was my intention. I always keep my word. Jennet here asked a young servant girl named Emma to pack a few of your personal belongings."

'Twas true, Constance thought. Lady Appleton did keep her word. Not always in a timely manner, but Constance told herself she must be grateful for whatever aid she got. It did her no credit to resent this, and to demand an explanation for Lady Appleton's long delay in responding to her letter would only harm her cause.

As Constance argued with herself, Lady Appleton turned her attention to Lucy. "I have also been to your cottage, Mistress Milborne. And to Canterbury."

Constance's hand clenched on the clean shift she'd

just removed from the capcase. Lady Appleton knew about Lucy. Would it make any difference? Would she now refuse to help them further?

Remembering things she'd heard long ago, Constance feared she might. Sir Amyas Leigh, Lady Appleton's father, had been a staunch supporter of the New Religion. He'd been long dead by the reign of Queen Mary, but many of his friends had gone into exile then, rather than pretend to convert to Catholicism.

As Adrian Ridley had.

Constance had herself been raised in King Henry's church and had served those high in power at the court of his son, Edward VI. And yet religion had never been a matter of great personal concern to her. Loyalty to her mistress had kept her at the marchioness's side during the bad times. Loyalty to Lucy, with whom she'd formed a bond of kinship and friendship during the last year, now obliged her to defend her cousin, no matter the consequences of Lucy's faith.

Lucy ignored Lady Appleton's comments. After a moment, she began to rock back and forth, back and forth, humming to herself. She gave an excellent impression of a madwoman.

With a shake of her head, Lady Appleton turned to face Constance. "There was once a Benedictine priory in Canterbury. Your cousin was a nun there until the dissolution of the monasteries."

"So I have been told. Has this any relevance?"

"I cannot think of any reason why having been a nun so many years ago, of itself, should lead to false charges of witchcraft now. Can you?"

"Most people do not think the charges are false."

"Most people have not read the published account of the witchcraft trials at Chelmsford last summer. Many of the things claimed against you two have been gleaned direct from those pages."

"How does that signify? One of the clergymen who examined me was present at that trial."

"Excellent. Then he will see—"

"He sees only what he wants to see. As, no doubt, the justices will, too. They will look at similarities and decide they exist because all witches behave in similar ways. Indeed, they seem to think all witches are in league with one another."

"Then we must make them realize that someone who read the pamphlet set out to incriminate the two of you. Logic dictates that this same person was the real culprit in the murders of two men."

Shocked out of her accustomed stillness, Constance took a step toward her. "But why? What does this person gain?"

It had occurred to Constance that someone had lied in order to cast suspicion on them, but what Lady Appleton suggested was far more evil, nothing less than a plot to bring Lucy's death and Constance's, too.

"What is to be gained? That is my question, also. If my theory is correct, your execution, or Lucy's, must benefit someone."

"And the two men who died?"

"Their deaths were but a means to an end."

Constance struggled to take in all the ramifications. One stood out. If Lady Appleton was right, then she, or Lucy, had indeed been the cause of Peter Marsh's death. Guilt assailed Constance, making her dizzy with remorse. She sagged against the stones. "All this. All Lucy and I have suffered. The deaths of two men. Because someone wanted us dead? I know no one who hates either of us that much."

"It is possible," Lady Appleton said, "that someone killed both men, then got the idea to cast blame upon the two of you, because either Clement Edgecumbe's death or that of Peter Marsh was what he, or she, desired. And yet, why choose you two?" She shook her head, as if she shared Constance's bewilderment. "Only one fact remains clear. The charges of witchcraft were deliberately created to conceal another crime, one which has naught to do with the supernatural."

"But no one has any reason to want me dead. Or Lucy."

"Are you certain?"

"And why kill Peter Marsh? He was no one. He had no kin. No heirs."

Lady Appleton reached out and touched Constance's forearm. "I believe it is time you told me the whole truth, Constance. There must be a reason why someone would think his death could be used to implicate you."

"He was not my lover!"

"But you knew him. Tell me about him."

Reluctantly, Constance let herself remember. Peter Marsh had been a well-favored fellow, sturdy of leg and arm and fair of face. He'd teased her unmercifully about her insistence upon sweeping out the rushes that covered the floors at Mill Hall every month, without fail, and replacing them with fresh ones. Most people made do with twice a year.

"Peter Marsh fancied himself attractive to women."

"Was he in truth?"

"Passing so," Constance admitted.

"Did he . . . court you?"

"Seduce me, you mean? No." But he had, she recalled, been different toward her just at the last. Speaking slowly, working it out as she went, she voiced her thoughts. "I always suspected that his talk of conquests was mere bragging, that he spouted nonsense to cover up a real affection for just one woman. Not me," she added quickly, seeing Lady Appleton's face. "And I felt no jealousy. Peter's greatest interest in me was as some-

one to whom he could boast about his latest scheme
for making money." The last time she'd spoken with
him, she'd thought he was up to no good. She wondered now if that had been what killed him.

"He was the sort of man who thrived on inventing
clever little schemes and for some reason, after Hugo
dismissed him, he seemed to have more money than
before. There was another odd thing, too. The last
time we met, he did behave in a different manner toward me."

"In what way?"

Constance felt herself color. She'd dismissed his
words as meaningless, but now they came back to
haunt her. "He said we'd make a good pair."

"You mean he suggested you marry?"

"I suppose he might have meant that. I did not think
him serious. He often teased me and he did not seem
any more sincere than he ever was. Even when he tried
to kiss me, there was no emotion behind it."

She remembered passionate kisses. Robert's kisses.
She knew how to tell the difference.

"You rebuffed him?" asked Robert's widow.

"Yes. He told me he would not give up. That I had,
of a sudden, become most attractive to him."

"Why would he say that?"

"A jest?" She'd assumed so at the time.

"Had someone else shown an interest in you? Could
he have thought he had a rival for your affections?"

"Adrian Ridley," Lucy said in a loud voice.
"Doubtless that is why he is now determined to convict me!"

"Did Ridley show an interest in you?" Lady Appleton
asked.

"No more than Peter Marsh. I am not the sort of
woman to inflame men's passions. Nor am I desperate

to wed." She met Lady Appleton's eyes and lowered her voice. "I loved once. It was enough."

An abrupt nod was all the acknowledgment she got. "Who knew you met with Marsh?"

"No one." Constance shifted her weight, of a sudden ill at ease. "We met beneath that wych elm," she admitted. "He chose the spot. He did not want Hugo to see us together after he left my cousin's employ."

"There was bad blood between them?"

"Not that I know of. He simply liked to keep secrets."

"Why did Hugo dismiss him?"

"Sir Adrian came. Hugo pinches pennies. He had no need for a clerk when his chaplain could take on those duties, too."

"And why did he have his own chaplain?"

"I would think you'd have guessed that, Lady Appleton. To convince all the world of how devout he is."

"To hide his true religion?"

"Oh, Hugo is as honest a churchgoer as you or I. But he has the mistaken conviction that rewards come from the appearance of excessive piety. He wants to be made a local justice."

"Your arrest cannot have helped his cause."

"No," Constance agreed.

"Did you know Hugo was courting Damascin Edgecumbe?"

The abrupt change of subject startled Constance, but the question itself took her completely by surprise. Hugo and Damascin? Although such a match made economic sense, she had difficulty imagining them in bed together. "He never spoke of this to me. But you have met him. You know he is uncommon close-mouthed."

Lucy had stopped rocking and was regarding Lady

Appleton with great curiosity. "Have you no questions for me? I knew Constance was meeting that fellow under the wych elm. I know other secrets, too."

"Do you know how the Edgecumbes acquired the land upon which Edgecumbe Manor was built?"

"They destroyed the property of mother church." Lucy's answer was prompt and accompanied by a sneer. "Lady Appleton of Leigh *Abbey*. You would know about such things. Your people were no better than Clement Edgecumbe."

"Lucy," Constance remonstrated, suddenly afraid that her cousin would go too far and end up driving Lady Appleton away.

That gentlewoman herself lifted a hand to silence Constance. She spoke to Lucy with her accustomed bluntness but no sign of rancor. "I understand why you must think so, but to debate what happened in my grandfather's time will not keep you from dancing the hempen jig on Penenden Heath." She glanced at Constance. "I learned one thing by visiting Lucy's cottage. Fine healthy banewort bushes grow near that wych elm. Edgecumbe and Marsh were not killed by witchcraft, but by poison."

Lucy chuckled. "I thought so myself but what profit in mentioning it? The authorities are determined to bring charges against us. Mention poison and they would only say that was the means we used."

"A witch, however, does have an advantage over a common felon. Upon conviction, felons lose their estates to the Crown."

"Do you mean someone stands to gain goods and chattel from our deaths?" Constance interrupted. "But neither of us has much to leave."

" 'Tis true," Lucy agreed. "When I entered the nunnery I gave up all secular claims and worldly goods."

"And when you came out again?"

"Like most of my sisters, I was granted but a pound a year to live upon. I returned to Mill Hall. Where else could I go? 'Twas my girlhood home, built by my grandfather. My father was still alive then."

"Who was his heir?"

"I had two brothers. One died young. The other had no children. When he died, seven years after our father, then Constance's father and Hugo's father, the sons of my grandfather's daughters, squabbled over the inheritance. I did not care who won, so long as I could continue to live in my cottage."

"My mother and father both died of the sweat three years later," Constance put in, remembering the pestilence that had swept the land toward the end of King Edward's reign. "So did Hugo's mother. After that, Miles Garrard moved into Mill Hall. He was the one who took me in when Lady Northampton died. Upon Miles's death last year, Hugo inherited."

"It is customary for men to lay claim to land and assume the responsibility for indigent female relations," Lady Appleton said. "It is unusual for a woman to inherit outright, unless there is a dearth of male heirs. Even then, a woman's husband is usually the one who holds title. And yet . . . who is your heir, Lucy? I do not suppose you have a will—"

"You suppose wrongly. I may not own much, but what I have I mean to have disposed of as I see fit. All I possess goes to Constance. Master Marsh helped me draw up the document."

This was news to Constance.

"She'll not be able to inherit if she is executed along with you. Has it occurred to you, Lucy, that Constance's best chance of surviving is to claim you are guilty and plead she was but an innocent bystander?"

The suggestion made Constance furious. "I will never turn against my cousin."

"Not even to save yourself? Then who inherits what you leave, Constance? Who is your heir?"

"I . . . I suppose everything will go to Hugo. There are no other relatives left. But you cannot mean to suggest that Hugo wants us both dead so he can inherit? He has sufficient for his needs and the wherewithal to catch a wealthy wife. Lucy has naught to leave but her books and clothing and household goods. Not even any chattel. And I have less than that."

"No one but Peter Marsh knew Constance was my heir," Lucy said.

"Marsh might have told someone."

"And are we to suppose that was the reason for his death? What you say makes no sense."

"Are you certain?"

That question again. Constance felt herself flush with anger. "I know one thing. In spite of her familiarity with banewort, Lucy did nothing. You were aware of this same poison without ever having used it against another. Can you not convince the justices of that simple fact?"

"Only if I can also show them that you are both innocent pawns in someone else's game. Otherwise, or so I am informed, I may end by putting my own head into the noose next to yours."

That bald statement left Constance momentarily speechless. She'd not considered that there was any great danger to Lady Appleton. That explained, she supposed, why the other woman had not come at once. Appalled at the risk she'd unknowingly asked Lady Appleton to take, Constance opened her mouth, then closed it again. What point now in apologizing for writing that letter, for pleading with her to involve herself in their troubles?

"Answer my questions, truthfully and completely," Lady Appleton said. "That is the way out for us all.

Let us work together to discover who had reason to concoct such an elaborate scheme. Someone stands to profit by one or more of four deaths." She turned again to Lucy. "There were no books in your cottage. Had you hidden them?"

Lucy's sudden mirth verged on hysteria. "They think to find spells in them."

Constance failed to see the humor. Between cures and spells there appeared to be little difference under the law.

Still sputtering, Lucy subsided enough to answer Lady Appleton. "The books were seized when I was arrested."

"So much for my inheritance," Constance murmured.

"I know my recipes." Lucy had missed the sarcasm. "I can write them again did I but have paper and ink and a good goose quill."

"I will provide those things," Lady Appleton promised. "I also want you to write down anything you can think of that may help me find out who is behind this sorry business."

" 'Twould do as much good to consult the nearest bed of lilies." Lucy chuckled and snorted.

"Lilies?" Confused, Constance looked to Lady Appleton for an explanation.

"I wish it were that simple," Lady Appleton said. "Your cousin refers to an old superstition that holds one can bring forth the clues necessary to solve any crime committed during the past year by burying an old piece of leather in a bed of lilies."

26

After two long hours of asking questions, Susanna left Maidstone gaol with no better sense of who might be behind Constance's troubles than she'd had when she went in. There seemed no reason for anyone to kill either Edgecumbe or Marsh, let alone cast blame on Lucy and Constance.

Finding a bed of lilies had a certain appeal. The dearth of clues and the nearness of the Assizes left Susanna in a quandary. She had only this evening and the next three days to discover the truth. If she did not, those two women would die.

At least, Susanna thought, she had solved one minor mystery. There had been no books or papers in Lucy's cottage because they had been confiscated by the constable when he'd come to arrest her for witchcraft.

"What now?" Jennet asked. Although she'd been with Susanna in the cell, she'd spoken not a single word during the visit. Susanna had surmised, from the wary glances Jennet darted at Lucy, that she feared to call herself to the old woman's attention.

Both the gaol and the Queen's Arms were in Maidstone's High Street. They were already in front of the inn.

"I need to confirm my suspicions about the use of banewort by speaking with Damascin," Susanna told her. "She saw Marsh's body. And I would learn if Hugo Garrard has arrived in Maidstone yet. Then there is the constable who confiscated Lucy's books and papers. I wonder if he had them sent here?"

She dispatched Jennet to the common room to give Fulke and Lionel their instructions, and continued on alone to her bedchamber. She hoped to find that a messenger had come from Canterbury with word from Master Calthorpe.

Someone had indeed paid a visit in her absence, but not to deliver a letter. Susanna surprised the intruder in the act of rifling her possessions.

"Do you seek something in particular, Mistress Baldwin?" She made the inquiry in her sweetest voice but, as soon as she was inside the chamber, she closed the door behind her and dropped the bar into place.

Winifred Baldwin whirled around. A snarl escaped her when she saw that Susanna had locked them in. "A mother has a right to protect her only son!"

"What harm do you imagine I intend him?"

The insinuation made her furious, but as she moved deeper into the room she grappled with her rising anger and contained it. This confrontation had been brewing for months. If she could stay calm and talk to Nick's mother, one rational being to another, perhaps she could ease the animosity Winifred Baldwin obviously felt.

Sunlight streamed through the open window. Voices carried plainly from the innyard below, making it seem as if they were surrounded by other people. For that reason, it did not occur to Susanna that she might have anything to fear from her visitor . . . until she got her first good look at Mistress Baldwin's eyes.

They were dark with hatred. Her nostrils flared. "What kind of love potion did you use on my poor boy? Was it the fruit of the mandrake? Powdered white thornapple?"

A sensation like cold fingers caressing the nape of her neck made Susanna shiver. The thornapple growing in her stillroom had not been acquired for that purpose. Indeed, the only aphrodisiac she knew of that used thornapple as an ingredient was intended to make a woman subject to a man's will, not the other way around.

"Admit it. You cast a spell on him."

"I do not make or use love potions. I do much doubt they have any effect."

"Do not play the fool with me. I know such magic works."

"Indeed?" It seemed to Susanna that Mistress Baldwin possessed considerably more information about aphrodisiacs than a respectable matron ought to. "How do you come by such knowledge?"

A sputter of outrage answered her. "Do not try to cast blame on me, you vile creature. You have bewitched my son."

"You know that is nonsense, Mistress Baldwin. Can we not sit down like two reasonable women and discuss why it is you so dislike me?"

This request produced not agreement, nor greater anger, but an inexplicable change in Mistress Baldwin's demeanor. She paled, staggered a bit, and had to cling to the bedpost for support. "By St. Frideswide's girdle. Never tell me you enticed my son with naught but your body and the erotic arts."

Color crept into Susanna's face. She did not know which charge to resent more. It required renewed effort to keep her voice level. "What is it you fear, Mistress Baldwin? That I mean to marry your son?"

"He is very wealthy."

"So am I." Susanna seated herself before the window

and gestured for Mistress Baldwin to sit beside her. As continued to happen more often than she liked, she forgot that her right hand had been burnt until the sudden movement reminded her of the injury.

If Mistress Baldwin noticed that Susanna winced, she did not comment on it. Nor did she accept the invitation to sit. "He's too good for the likes of you."

"I have no intention of marrying your son, Mistress Baldwin, and I have told him so repeatedly."

"But you are already his mistress. Do not trouble to deny it. That he is so besotted with you is as much a hindrance to his making a good marriage as having you already to wife." She sat down heavily on the edge of the bed. "All I want is for my son to make a suitable match."

Understanding burst upon Susanna and with it reluctant sympathy. Winifred Baldwin wanted her son to marry a woman young enough to give him heirs. His mother wanted to be a grandmother.

"Perhaps your prayers will be answered. Doubtless by the time Nick returns from his sojourn in Hamburg, he will have lost interest in me. Why, he may even meet someone else there, someone of whom you can approve."

Imagining Nick with a young bride was surprisingly painful. Distracted, Susanna almost missed seeing the peculiar expression that came over Mistress Baldwin's face.

"Hamburg? When does he go to Hamburg?" Her voice rose with every word until it was shriller than the cry of a herring gull.

"After the Assizes. Mistress Baldwin, I—"

But Winifred Baldwin was no longer listening. A militant light in her eyes, she stormed to the door and unbolted it, then swept out of the inn chamber. Susanna was left behind to stare after her in astonishment.

27

Winifred burst into her son's parlor without knocking. "Hamburg?" she demanded. "You are going to Hamburg? When did you plan to tell me? Can you imagine how mortified I was that I had to hear it from that woman?"

"Mother, calm yourself. I would have informed you of my plans soon enough. I'd scarce go off and leave you without making proper provision for your care."

"You can scarce go off at all when you are needed here."

"My presence in England is not essential. My presence in Hamburg will assure our future profits. It is necessary that I go."

Winifred glowered at him, but she knew full well the latest news from the Continent supported his argument. Even before Nick's father's death, she had made it her business to be informed of the fortunes of the Merchant Adventurers. Hamburg was vital to trade. If Nick went now, his interests there would be established for years to come.

"You leave after the Assizes?"

"Aye."

"How long will you be gone?"

"I cannot say. I do not mean to stay longer than necessary, but it may well be a matter of years rather than months." His slight smile seemed forced. "You'd best return to London in the interim."

He knew she hated country living, but he did not know why. He did not understand that she'd been able to escape rural poverty only by running away to London. He did not know that the girl she'd been then would have done far worse things than trap his father into marriage.

Life had taught Winifred to know the value of each item Bevis Baldwin traded and to keep a tight hold on every groat, too.

"I have been giving some consideration to leaving you in charge of the business while I am gone," Nick said. "You managed well on my behalf after Father died." Nick had been out of England then. On his return he'd lost no time taking up the reins himself.

Winifred did not reply. He spoke naught but the truth. She'd turned a tidy profit, too, and had resented it when she'd been made to feel she was no longer needed.

"I thought this news would please you."

"So it does." But not enough to reconcile her with his announcement that he meant to spend months, perhaps years, abroad. "I do not like losing you for an uncertain length of time and I do much mistrust those foreigners among whom you will live when you are on the Continent."

"Better the German states than Persia or Muscovy. Letters can reach me with considerable ease. We will not lose touch as we did the last time I traveled abroad."

"There is that." Cajoled into a better humor, she forced a smile. "And in Hamburg you will be away from that woman."

"Her name is Susanna."

"She is not for you, Nick. You need a young woman. Biddable. Fertile."

"I have asked Susanna to marry me."

"She turned you down." Even Winifred could hear the smug satisfaction that laced her voice.

"I believe I can convince her to change her mind." He seemed oblivious to his mother's dismay.

No bribe, she thought, not even arranging for her to run the business for him, could make up for the possibility that Susanna Appleton might one day step in and take her place.

As Nick elaborated on his plans, Winifred began to make a few of her own. She could not trust that woman to keep her word. Lady Appleton was simply playing a devious game. She only delayed accepting Nick's proposal, angling for some concession or other. After all, Winifred's son was a rare prize. Any woman, deep down, had to want to marry him.

That being the case, it was only a matter of time until Lady Appleton accepted Nick's proposal . . . unless Winifred found a way to stop the match.

She had discovered no love potion in Lady Appleton's chamber at the Queen's Arms, but with a bit of effort that lack could be remedied. She would arrange for Maidstone's constable to search the premises, Winifred decided, after she had planted sufficient evidence to prove Susanna Appleton dabbled in witchcraft.

28

Disappointment flashed across Susanna's face when she opened the door and saw Nick. "I hoped for Jennet. She left some time ago with Lionel and Fulke to search out the inn where Mildred and Damascin Edgecumbe lodge."

"If they are staying in a private house, your wait may be prolonged. Jennet is not the sort to come back before she discovers the information you've asked for."

"Keep me company, then," she invited. "I will tell you of the visit I paid to the gaol after church."

"Let us talk instead of the meeting between you and my mother."

Either she'd followed him when he'd visited Susanna the previous night, or she'd discovered their neighbor's presence by accident. Either way, Winifred Baldwin had known how to find the woman she thought such a bad match for her only son.

"She told you of our conversation?"

"Not in so many words but it was not difficult to guess she had seen you. No one else knows of my plan to go to Hamburg. Mother was most upset to learn I mean to leave England again."

"Yes."

"I told her I'd asked you to marry me and go there with me."

"Oh, Nick."

"I am tired of her meddling, Susanna." He took both her hands in his. "I am capable of choosing my own wife."

"Indeed you are. But I am not she." With gentle firmness, she extricated herself from his grip. "I told your mother that."

"She did not believe you."

"No." She began to pace. "She swore I was deceiving her. Swore most colorfully indeed and . . ." Susanna stopped in the middle of the bedchamber, looking thoughtful. "She swore by St. Frideswide. Nick, when your mother was a girl, she'd have been raised in the church of Rome."

"Aye." Wary, he waited for her to explain.

"She must be of an age with Lucy Milborne. And in her youth she may have had friends who entered convents. Do you think—"

Remembering what Susanna had already told him of the results of her visit to Canterbury, Nick supposed it was possible. "I can ask," he said, "but I must broach the subject with care."

"Because she will not acknowledge old friends who may still have Papist sympathies?"

"Because she will realize the question came from you."

Now it was her turn to touch him. Her hand on his arm, she gazed deeply into his eyes. "I do not want to cause more dissension between you. It is unlikely she knows anyone who would remember Lucy as a nun. Indeed, I am not certain Lucy's past has anything to do with her present troubles." Her expression turned rueful. "Thus far, I have not had much success in discovering who poisoned Marsh and Edgecumbe. It may be that Lucy *is* the guilty party."

"When I talk to Mother again I will inquire about old friends. What harm in it?"

"Thank you, my dear." She seemed to gather herself. Nick was about to slip his arm around her shoulders when she withdrew her hand and backed up a step. "Now, about your mother and me."

"Susanna, it matters not at all what she thinks." He kept pace with her retreat.

"But it does . . . when she has the right of it." She continued to back away from him.

Bewildered, he ended his pursuit. "The right of what?"

"Your . . . affection for me is keeping you from making a marriage and having a family. I will never remarry, Nick. And I am doubtless barren. You need sons to inherit all you have built."

"I'll leave it to Rosamond!"

"Robert's daughter?" Her eyes widened at the suggestion.

"Your daughter in all that matters. For your sake—"

"No, Nick." For some reason what seemed to him to be a generous offer appeared to upset her more than anything else he'd said. "Indeed, Rosamond is one more reason I cannot go with you to Hamburg, as wife or as mistress. I have an obligation to her."

"Bring her along."

Nick could have kicked himself as soon as he uttered the invitation. He did not, in truth, much care for Robert Appleton's bastard daughter. She reminded him too much of her father.

Releasing Susanna, he helped himself to some of the wine set out on a table by the window. As he drank, he glanced at her again. At the look in her eyes, he set the goblet down with a thunk. She was comparing him to Robert! He did not know which was worse, that or her determination to be noble.

In a futile attempt to rein in his temper, he kept some distance between them. "So, you mean to give up what we have because you think I will be better off without you. Dragon water!"

She flinched at the expletive, then had to fight a smile. "Nick, I—"

"Do not entertain any had-I-wist that after knowing you I could be content with some simpleminded girl of my mother's choosing. And where either you or my mother get the idea that I am incapable of making my own decisions is . . ."

Words failed him. In exasperation, he crossed the chamber and pulled her into his arms. Gratified by her instant response to his kisses, he continued in that vein for some time, until she at last pushed lightly at his chest to shove him away. He released her at once.

"Come with me to Hamburg, Susanna. Without you I will never be complete."

"Oh, Nick. I am tempted. So tempted." Sincerity rang in her voice and was reflected in the depths of her azure eyes. "But even if I could overcome all other reservations there still remains one unsurmountable barrier. I am afraid to go to sea."

Frustration rapidly turned back into irritation. He knew her too well to believe she was lying to him, and yet the idea of this woman fearing something so ordinary as to travel by water made no sense to him at all. She was the bravest person he knew, the most fearless when it came to doing what she thought was right.

"It is not just the first part of the journey that requires travel by water," she said. "I know from Walter's letters that even to reach Hamburg by an overland route, one must use the Dutch canal system as far as Leewarden before going on by road to Hamburg."

Nick's eyes narrowed. Walter Pendennis? Was he at the root of the problem? He, too, had once asked

Susanna to marry him. But they had been friends. Not lovers. Never as close as he and Susanna were. Nick consoled himself with that knowledge as jealousy ate at him.

By Great Harry, should not a woman cross the sea if a man meant enough to her? In the next instant he mocked himself for his own foolishness. If she was afraid, there had to be a reason for it.

"Have you always feared water?" he asked.

She hesitated. "I have always felt queasy when the water is rough."

"We are not speaking of simple seasickness."

"No. And it is not water I fear. Do you know how to swim, Nick?"

He nodded.

"So do I."

She'd managed to surprise him yet again. Most folk lacked that skill. Sailors made it a point of faith not to learn, convincing themselves that their ship would not sink but resigned to going down with her if she did.

"When I was not yet six years old, I was sent to visit my mother's family. She'd died when I was barely two. A boy cousin taught me how to stay afloat, and more, in a shallow part of the stream that flowed through Dodderidge land. I can also remember, as a child, making short journeys by boat. I was not afraid then. Indeed, I loved being out on the water when the day was fine."

"What happened to change that?"

"When I was twelve, I took ship with my father. He'd engaged a sturdy little craft to transport us from Gravesend along the coast of Norfolk."

Nick could sense the intense struggle she waged with herself to confide these details in him. Her face pale, her hands clenched into fists at her sides, she stared right through him. 'Twas clear she saw other times, other places, in her mind's eye.

"Even now, so many years later, it is difficult to think about what happened. My mother, sister, and grandparents had all died before I was ten, but my father was fit and strong. I did not expect to lose him, too. He should have lived many more years. Decades longer. Instead, the sea took him."

"You survived."

"I could swim."

Nick poured out a cup of strong wine and pressed it upon her. She took a sip, then set it aside.

"For a long time, I had nightmares about the shipwreck, but I was not aware there was anything else wrong with me. I avoided water before my marriage. I used the excuse of seasickness to continue to do so after I wed."

A fine trembling began in her limbs. Nick pulled her into his arms and hugged her tight. "You saw Robert drown, too."

"But he did not—"

"You thought he had." For some two years, she'd feared he had died when his small rowing boat capsized. That the truth was otherwise did not alter this telling fact.

"I can see why you would not relish the prospect of going to sea after such experiences. But perhaps the time has come to overcome your qualms. You are a strong-willed woman, Susanna."

"Will alone is not enough to overcome the panic." Her eyes had a desperation in them when she met his gaze. "Is there nothing you fear, Nick? Nothing that makes you break out in a sweat, even though you know in your heart that there is no need to be afraid?"

"I am not overfond of snakes, but—"

"There. You see. And some people have an irrational dread of thunderstorms. Or great heights. Or—"

"Leaving the house."

"What?"

Nick suddenly remembered a story he'd heard, years ago, in Persia. "There once was a man who was terrified to leave his own home. He had been a successful merchant, traveling far and wide to buy and sell. Without warning, he began to experience terrible fear did he so much as venture into the courtyard of his house. The marketplace was out of the question. Trembling and nausea and even pain assaulted him. Only by staying inside could he remain free of such symptoms."

From the expression on Susanna's face, she comprehended the significance of these similarities.

"This merchant was rich enough that he might have stayed within doors and let others do his bidding. For a time, he retreated to his bed, remaining there for days on end. But he was unaccustomed to inaction and soon decided he must overcome his fears. Every day he would venture a bit farther from his door until, after many months, he was once more in the marketplace. But no matter how much he wanted to cross to the other side of the village, he could not make himself go on."

"He gave up?" Susanna's disappointment was so intense that Nick took heart.

"He might have, but one day there was a fire. A building beyond the merchant's limitations was ablaze. Trapped inside was a young woman for whom this man felt deep affection. Forgetting his fear, he ran to her rescue. Only after she was safe did he realize what he had done. As simply as that, he was freed forever from the spell that had held him prisoner."

29

After Nick left, Susanna sat unmoving for a long time. Her reluctance to go to sea was not the result of any enchantment. Nor was it likely to be ended by an act of heroism.

But the possibility of learning by degrees to overcome terror did seem a sensible suggestion. If she could cross rivers, even travel downstream for a bit as long as there were riverbanks in sight on either side, then could she not do much more with . . . practice?

Susanna hated having this weakness. It seemed to her a great irony that she, who was so rational when it came to seeing through superstitions, should be laid low by a completely irrational reaction.

She thought back over four long years, to the hours just before Robert had vanished in that rowing boat. She'd had a good many shocks already by the time she was ferried across the mouth of Southampton Water in pursuit of her husband. She'd felt only the usual queasy stomach produced by a choppy surface. But after, following her return to Leigh Abbey, she'd begun to experience an odd and annoying nausea at the sight of any body of water.

There was no logic to it. When she'd received proof that Robert had not drowned, after all, then that should have been the end of it. Instead, she'd had to start carrying a supply of ginger root for even the shortest trip that involved a river crossing. The problem had gotten worse, not better, until she began to avoid ships, boats, and barges whenever she could.

What had at first been only annoying was now debilitating. If there *was* some way to overcome it, if her mind could be made to prevail over her body, then Susanna knew she must attempt the cure.

Her thoughts on the subject had progressed no further than a vague scheme to accustom herself to water travel in small increments when Jennet at last returned. Susanna welcomed the distraction of Constance's problems. Thinking about her own had made her head ache.

"We have found them," Jennet announced. "The Edgecumbes lodge at an inn called The Ship. As does Sir Adrian Ridley. And Hugo Garrard is expected on the morrow."

As Susanna had hoped, it had been more productive to send Jennet than to go herself. Jennet was able to blend into a crowd and pass unnoticed where her mistress, being uncommon tall and by her dress a gentlewoman, stood out.

"So, all of our suspects abide together. That is most convenient."

"All but Master Norden. There has been no sign of him in Maidstone."

"There will be," Susanna predicted. "And I warrant 'twill be soon."

30

Damascin Edgecumbe, Jennet decided, was a sly puss.

She wanted to speak alone with Lady Appleton every bit as much as her mother wished to keep them apart. When she'd caught sight of Jennet skulking about outside The Ship, she'd sent Margery, her maidservant, with a message. In response to it, both Jennet and Lady Appleton attended evening church services. So did Lionel and Fulke. Afterward, as they lingered in the nave, a heavily veiled figure, all in mourning black, approached them.

Black, and well she knew it, flattered Mistress Damascin's fair hair and pale skin. The maid who accompanied her also provided contrast, being plain-faced and dull brown in her coloring. Margery smiled shyly at Jennet and waited for her to step aside with her, leaving their mistresses to converse in private.

"I had not noticed such ostentatious mourning at Edgecumbe Manor," Jennet remarked.

Margery giggled. "Likes to dress up, does our Mistress Damascin. Playing at being the grieving widow, she is. For the nonce. More drama in it than being a girl who's lost her papa. Who can say who she'll be on the morrow?"

Childish games, Jennet thought. As she watched,

Margery's mistress lifted her veil. Her eyes were bright, curious, and somehow, although 'twas most like only a trick of the light, malevolent.

Lady Appleton must have suggested they leave the church, probably because the sexton was showing too much interest in their little party, for the two gentlewomen began to walk toward the inn where the Edgecumbes lodged. Jennet and Margery caught up with them just in time to hear Mistress Damascin ask after Lady Appleton's "poor hand."

She sounded sincere in her concern, but Jennet's protective instincts were roused by the reminder of what had happened at Edgecumbe Manor. Lady Appleton insisted the scalding must have been an accident. Jennet was not so certain.

"It is much improved," Lady Appleton said, and tugged off her glove to show skin that was peeling but otherwise normal.

"Mother will be . . . relieved."

"Will she?" Jennet muttered.

To her surprise, the young woman overheard the remark and responded with a trill of laughter as she turned to look at Jennet. "No. Indeed, she would be pleased to hear your mistress suffers mightily. She cannot approve of anyone who would champion Lucy Milborne."

"Why does she so dislike her neighbor?" Lady Appleton asked.

"Oh, that is easy enough. She has been jealous of old Lucy for years."

"Jealous?"

A yellow curl bounced free of Mistress Damascin's head-dress when she nodded. "My father wanted to marry Lucy Milborne when they were both young. She turned him down once to become a nun and again when she was no longer in holy orders."

"Why did she turn him down the second time?" Lady Appleton inquired.

"They could not agree on matters of religion, or so I was told. 'Twas long before I was born." Mistress Damascin's eyes were full of mirth as she and Lady Appleton resumed walking and once more left their servants to trail behind.

Jealousy, Jennet reflected, was a powerful emotion. Had it been enough to drive Mistress Edgecumbe to kill her own husband and place blame on the woman she thought had come between them?

Lady Appleton deftly changed the subject. "I am sorry if it pains you, Damascin, but the reason I wanted to talk to you was to ask you about Peter Marsh. I am told you were the one who found his body."

"Indeed, I did. And horrible it was, too."

"How did you come to be walking by the wych elm?"

"I was on my way to Mill Hall to meet Hugo." She turned her head sideways, allowing Jennet to see her expression, and sent a coy look Lady Appleton's way. "Did you know we are to be married?"

If there had been any doubt about a betrothal, neither Mistress Damascin's voice nor her manner betrayed it. She spoke as if the matter had been settled for some time. Jennet wondered if Garrard was wealthier than he seemed. She could not otherwise fathom his appeal for a young and beautiful woman.

"You went alone?" Lady Appleton asked. "Unescorted?" They were well along the High Street now, nearly at the place where they must turn to reach The Ship or go straight for the Queen's Arms.

Stopping, Damascin Edgecumbe faced her inquisitor. Her hands clenched into fists at her sides. "I do not like it when people try to keep me prisoner." A pout had crept over her face, souring her features.

Since it was Mistress Damascin's rebellious streak

that had led her to arrange this meeting, Lady Appleton did not reprove her, nor even point out that 'twas a dangerous route to take if she'd believed the witch who'd killed her father lived hard by the path between the two houses. Instead, she inquired as to the condition of Marsh's body. Jennet stretched her ears to hear the reply.

"He was dead." Her voice was flat. Emotionless.

"Did you turn him over? He was lying facedown, I am told."

"I thought I could help him, but I saw at once I was too late." She lowered her head to contemplate her hands, which were now held clasped in front of her.

Jennet moved closer, intent upon getting a better look at the young woman's face.

"But you did recognize him?" Lady Appleton prompted. "You knew Peter Marsh?"

She nodded. "He called upon my father many times."

"When he was still in Garrard's employ?"

"Then and after." She glanced up, from beneath her lashes. "He said he loved to have an excuse to visit Edgecumbe Manor because I was there. But Mother never did like him. She sent him away the one time he showed up after Father died."

"A handsome man?"

"He was when he lived. Dead he was grotesque." With an exaggerated shudder, she began to walk again, choosing the way that led to The Ship. "His legs and arms sprawled without dignity. His dead eyes were open and staring. 'Twas most disturbing."

But she did not sound distressed to Jennet. She sounded as if the sight of the body had fascinated her as much as it had repulsed her.

"Did you note the pupils?" Lady Appleton asked.

"I did not tarry to inspect the corpse in any detail."

She quickened her pace. "I was grievous sick and then I ran home to Mother."

"And what did she do?"

"She sent our steward for the constable."

"And?"

"I told him what I'd found and he went and looked at the body. Then Mother gave me poppy syrup to calm me and I slept the remainder of the day."

"You must know something more." Lady Appleton put one hand on Mistress Damascin's arm, but her quarry did not slow down. They were almost back at the inn.

"What more could I know?" Mistress Damascin sounded impatient.

"Something must have happened by that evening to convince the authorities that Marsh was bewitched, and that your father had been also. By nightfall, both Constance Crane and Lucy Milborne had been arrested and charged with those crimes. If you did not make the first accusation, who did?"

They had reached the innyard. The young woman now seemed anxious to get away. "Mother did. She knew from the first that Father had been bewitched. And by whom. She only hesitated to accuse Mistress Milborne for fear the old witch would cast an evil spell on me in retribution."

Jennet saw Lady Appleton's eyebrows lift. "Then you believe witchcraft was the cause of these men's deaths?"

"Why, what else could it have been?"

"Plain murder, mistress."

If Lady Appleton expected some reaction to this charge, she was disappointed. Mistress Damascin was no longer paying attention. Her gaze shifted to something behind Jennet and Margery, and she smiled with genuine amusement. "Oh, look. There is that silly fellow who was wont to follow me about like a lovesick sheep. I wondered what had become of him."

By the time Jennet turned, there was no one in sight. "What fellow is that?" Lady Appleton asked.

"His name is Chediok Norden. A man well grown now," she added in a thoughtful voice, "but as a boy he was in service at Egdecumbe Manor."

"A servant lad?"

"Aye." Mistress Damascin preened. "He thought I was uncommon pretty."

Jennet could not deny that the young woman had the sort of looks men fancied, but she also had an inflated opinion of herself. Any sensible fellow would find that trait most unappealing.

"Did Norden know Lucy Milborne?" Lady Appleton asked.

"You might say so. Once, I remember, he threw rocks at her house on a dare. One broke a glass window. She was most annoyed at him."

No doubt she had been. Glass was expensive. Expecting to hear that Mistress Milborne had put a curse on Chediok Norden, or had him arrested, Jennet was surprised when Mistress Damascin proceeded to claim credit for instigating his act of vandalism. "He thought to impress me with his bravery by taunting a known witch."

For the first time, Jennet wondered if she'd been wrong about Lucy Milborne. Surely a witch with any power at all would have known of the young woman's involvement and taken revenge—by sending the morphew to mar her complexion, mayhap. Or tormenting her with something else exceeding nasty. Boils on the buttocks. Griping in the guts. A disfiguring cast to one eye.

"Have you talked to Chediok Norden during the last

few weeks?" Lady Appleton asked, interrupting Jennet's speculations.

"Oh, no. It has been years since I last saw him."

"He did not come to Edgecumbe Manor to ask questions?"

"If he did, Mother must have turned him away. She never did like him."

A chill crept up Jennet's spine at the words. Mistress Damascin had said the same thing about her mother's feelings toward Peter Marsh.

31

As soon as Damascin and her maid went inside the inn, Susanna beckoned to Fulke and Lionel. "There was a young man following us. Did you notice him?"

Fulke nodded.

"Good. Find him and persuade him to visit me at the Queen's Arms."

With two stout fellows to enforce his cooperation, Chediok Norden soon became Susanna's guest. She sat in the chamber's single chair. Norden took a stool. The others remained standing.

"I am told you were once a servant at Edgecumbe Manor." She made a *tsk*ing sound. "You lied to us, scribbler."

"She remembered me?" Hectic color suffused his cheeks.

"Why did you leave your post there?"

"To better myself. To become wealthy."

"You were not sent away?"

"Nay."

Susanna was not sure she believed him. Not after what she'd heard from Damascin.

Questions about Peter Marsh and Hugo Garrard and Clement Edgecumbe yielded no information she did not already have. Norden proved passing unobservant for a man who claimed he meant to make his living by describing people and events.

"Where have you been since we last saw you?"

Norden hesitated, then appeared to decide there was no harm in telling her. "To Bethersden and Boughton Monchelsea." With sudden eagerness, he leaned toward Susanna, ignoring the fact that Fulke moved closer, alarmed by the abrupt movement. "I sought links between Mother Milborne and the others who stand accused as witches."

So, like the clergymen, he thought he would find connections. More sensational details for his pamphlet. "You are a menace to all women," she told him, "even your beloved Damascin."

"Not Damascin. She is pure and fine."

"And her mother?" Jennet asked.

Norden gaped at her. "Have you learned something? Is she a witch, too?" A hopeful gleam appeared in his eyes.

"A poisoner, perhaps," Susanna told him, "but not a witch. Nor is Lucy Milborne. Use the brain God gave you, Norden. If there were as many witches as you seem to think, their presence would have been detected long before this."

"They are clever." He nodded, sure of himself and then, before Susanna's eyes, belatedly leapt to a foolish conclusion. She could not have been more sure of it had he spoken his thought aloud. His eyes widened in sudden fear. He trembled and turned pale and swallowed so hard that his Adam's apple bobbed.

Resigned to the fact that she'd get no more out of him, unless she chose to lie and confirm his obvious misapprehension and frighten him into some further revelation, Susanna sighed.

"No, Norden," she said with as much firmness as she could muster. "I am not a witch, either."

32

It was not difficult to discover where one might purchase a love potion but getting there required dedi-
cation. Winifred crossed Maidstone's bridge to the
west bank of the Medway. There were few buildings,
except around the hospital, and as she made her
way upriver she encountered only scattered signs of
habitation.

In this direction, the river was navigable by small
vessels for another five miles, but the passage of larger
ships was obstructed by a series of weirs and fulling
mills. The clay called fuller's earth was plentiful in
these parts. Tall, prickly teazles, used for raising the
nap on woolen cloth, grew in great abundance.

A mean hovel had been erected near the riverbank
a mile from the town. Winifred had no doubt this was
her destination. It did much resemble the place, built
into the corner of what had once been a London garden, where she had bought the charm she'd used on
Bevis. She wrinkled her nose at the stench of the lay-
stall in front and came close to changing her mind
about entering.

This was worse, she thought, than any place in London. At least, in the city, the raker blew his horn before

every door on Mondays, Wednesdays, and Fridays, to remind citizens to bring their offal out into the open streets and throw it into the channels that ran down their middles, there to be washed away with buckets of water drawn from the householders' wells. There were days it took more than a dozen bucketfuls from each to do the job, but it did get done. Maidstone and its environs would do well to enact similar regulations on their rubbish and dunghills.

Winifred was honest enough, however, to allow that London was filthy in other ways. Vaults and latrines hanging over the town ditches turned the water below black. Dead animals floated there, too. Pudding-wives and tripe-wives threw out paunches, guts, and entrails, which did not always wash away. A few of the city's rakers were not as diligent as their fellows about carrying away dirt and refuse before six in the morning. And some butchers were a disgrace, throwing offal into both street and ditch while blood ran in streams from the slaughterhouses in the Shambles. Kites, carrion crows, and ravens did more to clean up after them than the rakers did.

The direction her thoughts had taken did nothing to shore up Winifred's courage, but she was here now. She told herself she might as well go in.

Bracing herself to face the unknown, she pushed aside the curtain that served as a door and stepped into the cunning woman's lair. Two homely, prick-eared shepherd's curs looked up from their places on either side of the entry but neither barked. One lolled on the dirt floor, offering up his stomach to be scratched. The other bared his teeth.

Both smelt of dead things they'd rolled in. Combined with the odors of musty grain and tainted fish, it was enough to make Winifred's stomach turn and have her thinking again of retreat.

"Had a warner once," a low voice declared.

Winifred squinted through the dust motes and made out a small, wizened woman sitting in an enormous carved chair. "A warner?"

"A mongrel sort of dog. Good for naught but to bark and give warning when anyone stirred in the night season."

"It is morning." Winifred felt a sense of unreality. The conversation made no sense.

"Aye. But you've time to do your business here. I'll wait until noon to gather the leaves and flowers of the blessed thistle. Needs must be done on a dry day."

"I've come for a love philtre." Even to her own ears, Winifred's voice sounded strangled.

"Such things are expensive."

"I've money."

They settled on a price without much haggling, and a few minutes later Winifred was on her way back to Nick's house, a small vial hidden in her pocket.

Her step grew jaunty as she neared the bridge. Her plan was simple. It was not necessary that Susanna be arrested or charged with any crime. It would be enough if Nick found this evidence of her scheming hidden among her possessions. Later this day, Winifred would slip into Susanna Appleton's chamber at the Queen's Arms and secrete the vial somewhere it would not at once be noticed. The difficulty lay in making sure Nick thought to look where Winifred had hidden it, but she was confident she would contrive some way to manage that. Once he found the love potion, tangible proof that woman had used unnatural means to win his affection, he'd have no choice but to heed his mother's warnings.

Afterward, she supposed, he would need time to mend his wounded pride. Perhaps the length of his trip to Hamburg would accomplish that purpose. But when he returned, he would be ready to settle down. She intended to have a suitable young woman all picked out for him.

So intent was Winifred on her own thoughts that she did not notice until too late that a man was close behind her. She'd just reached for the latch on Nick's gate when a heavy hand clamped down on her arm.

Annoyed at such presumption, she turned with a glare that should have turned him to stone. "By St. Frideswide's girdle! Unhand me, sirrah."

He loomed over her, scarecrow thin, eyes bright with satisfaction as he murmured, "Got you."

"What means this effrontery?" And why did no one come to her rescue? The street was uncommon deserted. Winifred began to regret that she'd chosen secrecy over safety and taken no servant with her on the morning's errand.

"I will release you, madam, when you have made a decision."

"What decision?" Winifred was too annoyed to feel truly afraid, especially when the fellow stumbled over his threatening words.

"You have two choices. You can invite me in to discuss Lady Appleton's future, or I can call the constable and have him arrest you. You purchased a love potion, madam. The use of enchantments to procure love is against the law."

Winifred felt her jaw tighten. She selected a third option—to bluff. "You talk nonsense, young man."

"Do I? Let us go within and discuss how you can persuade me to keep silent." He stuttered the last word.

This evidence of further nervousness no longer did much to ease Winifred's mind. Her heart beat too fast and the vial seemed to have doubled in weight. She had the brief irrational thought that this rude fellow could see it through the heavy fabric of her kirtle.

"I mean what I say. I will give evidence against you."

There was doubtless some excuse she could make for her purchase. A reluctant dog she wished to breed, mayhap. But if claims were made against her in a public forum, that would ruin her plan to discredit Susanna Appleton. Worse, such talk might cause Nick's fellow merchants to turn against him, and if business fell off economic ruin would surely follow.

This was not the time, Winifred decided, to quibble over whether she had committed any crime by buying the potion. Thanks to Nick's current preoccupation with the statute on witchcraft, she understood all too well that the line was passing thin between what was criminal and what was not.

"Best come in," she told the stranger, taking comfort in the fact that, once they were inside, she'd have stout servants to call upon for help.

Nick's men could subdue her unwanted guest if that became necessary. Unfortunately, Winifred could also think of a great many disadvantages to asking for their assistance. She could scarce order them to kill this impertinent fellow, and if she had him thrown out, Nick would be sure to hear of the to-do. Even if the stranger did not carry through with his threat to accuse her, that could undo her scheme.

The house had been built on a terrace, raised above the garden by a low wall and steps. Winifred entered through the main door on the long side of the two-and-a-half-story building, which opened into a small entryway. The hall, and beyond that the kitchen, were off to one side. The parlor was on the other. They could be more private in the latter.

"What do you want of me?" she demanded when they were alone with the door barred.

"My name is Chediok Norden. I have reason to know of the connection between your son and Lady Appleton, and I have been keeping an eye on the old woman you visited this morning."

Winifred listened in growing alarm as he described how he had peered in through the window of the cunning woman's hovel and seen her exchange a gold coin for the love philtre.

"Lies! I shall call Nick's henchman and have you thrown into the street if you do not leave at once."

"If you were to call in your servants, Mistress Baldwin, they would do naught but bear witness to what I can find on your person. Do you want to spend a year in gaol for possessing what is in that vial? Something you bought from a witch?"

"No witch. A cunning woman only, skilled with herbs."

"She's more than that."

"What has this to do with Lady Appleton?" Winifred demanded, once more going on the offensive. It was intolerable to her that this scrawny young man should seek to master her.

"Lady Appleton is also much more than a skilled herbalist. I believe she had a hand in the murders with which those two gentlewomen in Maidstone gaol are charged."

Startled, Winifred abruptly sat, dropping her bulk into the bobbin-frame chair with such force that it creaked alarmingly. "How can you think so? Lady Appleton was miles away, in her own home, when those men died."

"Distance makes no difference to a witch. Did you know that she and Mistress Crane once shared a lover?"

Winifred gasped. "I thought the woman immoral, but your claim exceeds my darkest suspicions."

"Is it such a difficult choice to make, Mistress Baldwin? Help me to convict a witch."

"Help you how?"

"Go ahead with your plan—oh, yes, I have guessed what you plan to do with that potion. 'Twas not difficult to put together the pieces. You mean to hide that love philtre in her chamber."

"I did not intend to accuse her of a crime for which she could be executed!" Nick would never forgive her if she did that.

"She deserves death. They all do."

"But she had naught to do with—"

"Even if she did not, she attempts to free those who did and cast blame elsewhere. I cannot allow that."

The man was mad, Winifred thought. How could he think she would help him?

But how could she not do as he wished? It was a choice between Susanna and herself.

It was true that Susanna dabbled in potions, she assured herself, wanting to be convinced. Norden might be right. She could be a witch.

Her original plan *had* been to notify a constable and persuade him to search Susanna's room. When the authorities found the vial, Susanna would not be implicated in murder. She would face only a year in gaol. She was young and healthy enough to survive the sentence.

Winifred herself was not.

Imprisonment would kill her, and that would be her fate if Norden carried out his threat. Better to risk upsetting Nick, she decided. He'd get over it soon enough. Once he'd been faced with the proof of his mistress's evil ways, he'd realize he was well rid of her.

"I will hide the vial," she told Norden, "but naught else."

"It is enough. Send me word when the deed is done."

"No. No messages or messengers." She did not trust him. "I will be on the church porch at dusk if I succeed in doing as I've promised."

"As you wish. That will be my signal to alert the authorities. She'll be in gaol alongside her friends by tomorrow."

And she, Winifred realized with a surge of relief might thus escape all blame. Nick did not have to know what she had done.

That hope faded when, only moments after Norden's departure, Nick came into the parlor.

"Who was that just leaving?" he asked.

Of a sudden, Winifred felt old, too aged and infirm even to attempt to rise from her chair. Nick had seen Norden. When Susanna was arrested, he might make the connection.

Her only course seemed to be to tell him as much of the truth as she dared. "His name is Norden. He is in Maidstone because of the witch trials."

"What did he want here?"

Winifred hesitated. "He is aware of Susanna Appleton's interest in the matter and he found out that she is our neighbor. He sought me out to learn more about her."

Nick swore.

"Send her away." The impulsive suggestion was out before Winifred could stop it, for deep down she knew that hurting Susanna would hurt Nick, too.

"She'll not leave Maidstone without good reason."

"I feel it in my bones that this Norden intends to make trouble for her."

"You may be right, but Susanna will never agree to abandon the women in gaol. Besides, where could she go that will be any safer?"

Winifred opened her mouth and closed it again. Nick was right. There was no sanctuary. Short of encouraging her son to spirit Susanna Appleton off to Hamburg with him, she could not protect her from what was to come.

"I have decided to assist Susanna in finding out the truth." Nick gave Winifred a sharp look. "Do you care about the truth, Mother?"

Offended, she bristled, but she did not reply.

"If you do, you may be able to help me."

"How?"

"Lucy Milborne was once a nun. It would be helpful to locate someone who knew her in those days." He made a vague gesture. "She is of an age with you. Did any of your childhood friends enter nunneries?"

Winifred disliked remembering her childhood and she had no strong desire to help Susanna Appleton assist the women accused of being witches, but she could not deny her only child. "There were three that I remember."

"All from Croydon?"

His startled look amused her. "Back then, the religious life was a popular choice, more appealing than marriage for many girls. A gently or nobly born nun might hope to rise to a position of power, to become prioress or abbess."

"What nunneries did they enter?"

Pursing her lips as she sought distant memories, Winifred was surprised by how much she did recall. "One went to Syon. One was in the house of the Minoresses without Aldgate."

"And the third?"

"The Benedictine priory of St. Sepulchre in Canterbury." Winifred frowned as another scrap of her past came back to her. "That was the place that embraced the teachings of the Nun of Kent."

"And they had Lucy Milborne among their numbers." Eyes gleaming, excitement in his voice, Nick came and knelt by her chair. "Tell me all you know about the woman who went to St. Sepulchre's. Where can I find her?"

One hand went to his cheek. "I cannot guess where she is, Nick, or even if she is still alive. It has been over thirty years since the nunneries were closed and even before that I'd lost touch with all my childhood acquaintances."

"I know you do not like to be reminded of your life in the country, but do you think someone in Croydon might be able to tell me where she is?"

"You would go there?" Her hand stilled in the act of brushing a curl away from his face.

"Aye. Why not?"

Because, Winifred thought, she did not relish having him see the place from which she'd fled at such a tender age. And yet, it might be a good thing for him to go away from Maidstone just now. If he was in Croydon when she carried out her part of the bargain with Chediok Norden, he'd be less apt ever to learn of her role in Susanna Appleton's downfall.

"The woman's name was Phyllis Wynnington." A faint smile played about her lips. An elegant name for a plain girl. Her friends had made sport of it.

Nick rose to go to his writing table and withdraw a sheet of parchment.

"I thought you meant to look for Phyllis in person."

"This note is for Susanna." He did not look up from his scribbling.

In haste, Winifred schooled her features to hide her reaction. She must be careful not to reveal what she was thinking. Nothing must delay Nick's departure.

A few minutes later, he'd finished composing his missive. Sealing the letter, he summoned young Toby

to take it to the Queen's Arms, then bade farewell to
Winifred and went off to pack the few things he would
need for his journey.

As soon as Nick left the parlor, Winifred hastened
after the servant lad. Her agility fully restored, feeling
more vigorous than she had in days, she caught up
with him on the terrace steps.

"I will take this to Lady Appleton myself." She
snatched the letter from his hand.

This would provide the perfect excuse, should she
be caught hiding the love potion in Susanna's chamber.

33

When Hugo Garrard's arrival in Maidstone was reported to Susanna, she at once sent a message to Nick, hoping he would be able to strike up an acquaintance with Constance's cousin. Lionel returned a short time later, still carrying her unopened letter.

"Master Baldwin has left town."

"Without a word to me?" She could not help but feel hurt. True, Nick was not accountable to her for his whereabouts, but he must know that she would worry when she was unable to reach him. That she'd not appreciate Nick being concerned about her, were their positions reversed, added an element of irony to her reaction. She smiled ruefully at herself.

"I know where he's gone," Lionel offered. "Master Baldwin's man, Simon, told me. He went to talk to a nun. In Surrey."

This intelligence eased her worry, and she was glad to hear that Nick was acting in aid of her cause, but the hurt feelings, irrational as they were, remained.

She was, she decided, capable of talking to Hugo on her own, but she just missed catching him at The Ship. No one there knew where he'd gone, and Mildred and Damascin were also out.

"His man is in the common room," Fulke reported. "He has been there some time and has imbibed a good deal of beer. He had a falling out with his master and took a clout on the ear when he went too far with plain speaking."

Susanna considered this. "I believe I will sample The Ship's fare," she announced. "It is close to time for dinner."

A few minutes later, she was seated with Jennet, Fulke, and Lionel at a table in the common room and had given their order to a blue-coated boy. The food was comparable to that offered at the Queen's Arms. Both inns served assorted meat pies and cheeses along with beer, wine, and ale.

Arthur Kennison, his back to them, occupied a nearby table, but he was not alone. Chediok Norden had joined him during the time it took Fulke to fetch Susanna. Neither man noticed the quiet arrival of the party from Leigh Abbey.

Fulke had been right. Kennison was deep in his cups. With blatant intent to listen, Susanna edged her stool closer and canted her head in that direction.

"At least I am reliable," Kennison grumbled.

"Master Garrard should not have struck you." Norden drank deep as he commiserated.

"Garrard's last messenger wanted the prize for hissel. I've no interest in her."

Norden made a small, choked sound. "What say you?"

"Catched her, too, I warrant. At least for a quick futter."

"You blacken a good woman's name."

Kennison's inebriated chortle drowned out Norden's sputter of protest. "You are a fool if you think that one virtuous. And you should know better. You lived amongst them in that household, once upon a time."

Damascin? And did he mean Peter Marsh when he

spoke of Garrard's previous messenger? Stunned by the possibilities, Susanna turned to stare at the two men. The small scraping noise her stool made caught Norden's attention.

"Lady Appleton!" Eyes wide, he stared at her. "You. Here."

The urge to slap some sense into the fellow was strong, but she managed to restrain herself. Instead she addressed Kennison. "Where has your master gone?"

"Know not. Care not."

Cup-shot, he was no good to her, but even as she came to that conclusion, Hugo Garrard himself entered the common room of The Ship. He looked startled to find Kennison, Norden, and Susanna together but was quick to recover himself.

"Lady Appleton. Well met. I understand you have some knowledge of healing herbs. My cousin has need of you, for she is grievous sick."

"Constance?"

"Nay. Lucy. I have just been to see her in Maidstone gaol and though I know little of fevers and such, it seems to me that she is like to die."

34

The fever had come on during the night and by noontide Lucy was raving. Constance had bathed her forehead and forced her to gargle with ale to cool her mouth, and to drink liquids, but nothing seemed to help.

"She needs medicine," Constance shouted at the guard.

He ignored her, as he had all along.

She prayed Hugo would send help but dared not rely upon his good will. When they were first arrested, she'd thought he believed in her innocence. She'd trusted him to help them, but in truth he'd done as little as possible. He could not quite abandon them to their fate, being head of the family, but after his long silence, his visit earlier that morning had surprised her. Until then, he'd seemed content to use Adrian Ridley as his go-between.

As soon as he'd realized Lucy was ill, he'd beat a hasty retreat, fearing infection. 'Twas not gaol fever, Constance told herself. She hoped it was not Lucy's old malady returning, either.

The previous winter, after a similar fever, Lucy had experienced great trouble breathing. There had been a terrible wheezing sound in her chest. Without a still-room, without Lucy's own remedies, Constance feared that this time her cousin would not recover. Even with them, Lucy had not been herself again for months after that last fever finally abated.

Constance replaced the damp cloth on Lucy's brow and wondered if she had it wrong. Would it be a blessing, since they appeared destined to die on the gallows in a few days' time, to cheat the hangman?

The door creaked open behind her. Glancing over her shoulder, Constance saw that Susanna Appleton had arrived.

She was not alone. Adrian Ridley came in behind her, as did the servant, Jennet, carrying a basket. Lady Appleton wasted no time. She examined the feverish woman, then reached into the basket, which contained an assortment of herbs and fresh water. With a dexterity Constance could only envy, the gentlewoman measured and mixed and held the result to Lucy's lips.

"When Hugo described Lucy's symptoms to me," Lady Appleton said as she worked, "I went direct to the apothecary and the grocer for supplies. Centaury with water for fever." She helped Lucy to swallow the tonic by rubbing her finger on the older woman's throat. "Later I will send sage steeped in boiling water and a little betony and she can drink that."

"Father!" Lucy cried. Her fevered eyes were wide open, but there was no sense in them.

"She often calls out to her father when she is out of her mind with fever. She also shouts curses at her brother." In spite of her anxiety, Constance felt a slight smile curve her lips upward. "I do not think they were over-fond of each other."

"Tell me about them." Lady Appleton continued to minister to the sick woman. "What do you know of Lucy's family?"

"There is not much to tell. I never met them. I scarce knew mine own parents. I have heard that

Lucy's father was indulgent, her brother indifferent. He ignored her for the most part after her return from Canterbury, taunting her with the fact that she was less suited than he to run Mill Hall. He may have been right. She never showed any interest in housekeeping."

"Is this the same illness you nursed her through last winter?"

"Not so serious. Not yet." Constance described Lucy's symptoms and the treatment, which Lucy herself had directed in her lucid moments. "We were after more of the herb that cured her the night Peter Marsh died."

Constance would have continued to hover while Lady Appleton ministered to her cousin had Adrian not taken her by the arm to lead her a little apart, away from the smells of the herbs and the stench of the sick woman's sweat.

"Let her tend Lucy for a time. We are only in the way."

"*You* are in the way. Why are you here? If she dies, you cannot give her last rites."

"Would you want me to?"

Exasperation and exhaustion combined to make Constance careless of her words. "Yes! Why not give comfort? There was a woman in Lady Northampton's service who clung to the old ways, though the Northamptons were most assuredly followers of the New Religion. Since this woman did not have the good fortune to die during Mary Tudor's reign, Lady Northampton herself arranged to bring a Roman Catholic priest to her. Was that wrong?"

To judge by Adrian Ridley's shocked expression, it had been very wrong indeed.

Driven to madness by his manner, she shouted at him. "I have done worse things than that!"

"What things?"

"I fornicated with a married man."

Appalled, he backed up a step.

Belatedly remembering whose husband Robert Appleton had been, Constance flushed.

"How many others?" he demanded. "How many other men have you seduced?"

She was tempted to say a hundred. A thousand. Instead she told him the simple truth. "There was no other man after that one. For all his flaws, I loved him and was faithful to him."

"She speaks the truth, Sir Adrian," Lady Appleton said. "She'd have married him if he'd had the strength of character to defy his overlord and refuse to wed me."

"Your husband was—?"

"Constance's lover. Yes. And I have long since looked past that fact, as you must, Sir Adrian." She gave a wry, self-deprecating laugh. "Why not? Constance was not Robert's only mistress. And at least she did not present him with a child."

Constance felt her mouth go dry. A child? Robert had a child?

"Lucy will have no need of last rites." Lady Appleton stood and began to return items to her basket. She spoke, no doubt of medications, but Constance no longer heard a word of it.

Adrian had taken both her hands in his. "Do you swear to me that you did not lie with Peter Marsh?"

"Why should I? He could not compare to Robert Appleton. No man can. And I did not kill him, either. Nor did Lucy have any reason to want Clement Edgecumbe dead."

"I have been told he loved her once but that she rejected him, reviling him for stealing the property of mother church."

"Love and hate, Sir Adrian, are ofttimes difficult to

distinguish from one another. Lucy and her former suitor did both enjoy their quarrels. She lamented his death."

Constance had not previously thought of the relationship between Lucy and Edgecumbe in quite that way, but 'twas true. They had engaged in spirited debates, sparring with each other on any and all topics, never in agreement.

Not unlike the way she and Adrian clashed.

35

TUESDAY, JULY 8, 1567

Nick had ridden hard, thanking his stars that his mother had not been born and bred in Cornwall or Northumberland. But even to reach Croydon in Surrey, some thirty miles from Maidstone, he'd dared not delay, not even long enough to stop and talk to Susanna before he left. Not if he was to question Phyllis Wynnington and return in time to do anyone any good. The Assizes began on Thursday with civil cases. The witches and other felons would be tried on Friday.

His horse had thrown a shoe, delaying him so that he'd been obliged to spend the previous night at Kenton, some miles short of his goal. In the early morning he'd ridden on and now, just past noon, it seemed his luck, at last, was in. Ahead was the cottage of Mistress Wynnington, now Mistress Comstock, mother of five and grandmother of dozens. She still lived in Croydon.

The tiny, birdlike woman was at first reluctant to admit she had once been a nun. Nick understood. There were many who felt a lingering prejudice against Catholics after Queen Mary's blood-soaked reign.

"Everyone in Croydon must know your history," he reminded her.

"The question I ask is how you came to know it."

"My mother is a native of this place. Her name was Winifred Marley before she wed my father."

"Winifred Marley! I thought she died years ago."

"She is alive and well and living, for the most part, in London."

"Tell me all," Mistress Comstock demanded. "I would have a full account of your mother's life after leaving Croydon."

"In return, will you tell me all you remember about Lucy Milborne?"

The deep lines in her face became still more starkly incised as Mistress Comstock tried to call Lucy to mind.

"She came from Kent. Near Hythe. A place called Mill Hall."

"Near Aldington?"

"Aye."

Fear flickered across Mistress Comstock's features. She studied Nick's face with intent, beady eyes. "Why do you want to know about her?"

"She is accused of a crime. It is possible she was charged not because she is guilty but because of something that happened long ago, when she was a nun. Anything you can recall about her could help save her life."

Trust came hard, but at length Mistress Comstock admitted she did remember one thing—Lucy had reacted to every crisis with an excess of emotion most unseemly in a nun.

"She was prostrate with grief for weeks afterward when word came that Elizabeth Barton was dead."

The Nun of Kent. Nick knew the story. Elizabeth Barton had been convicted of treason, executed not for her religion, or even for claiming to have had visions, but for daring to tell the king he had sinned. It would not have been safe back then to seem to sympathize with her, or to mourn her. Even now, a kind word about her might be taken the wrong way.

"Lucy must have been distraught when they evicted her from the priory."

"Oh, yes," Mistress Comstock agreed. "I do remember that. Well-nigh raving, she was. Foolish talk. Claimed they'd ruined us." She chortled. "Throwing us out into the world was the best thing that could have happened to us, I say. Look at me, Master Baldwin. Do I look ruined?"

"Indeed, madam, you seem both prosperous and happy."

"And so I am."

Nick knew only what little Susanna had been able to tell him of Lucy's life. He had not met her. He had no idea if she was a madwoman or a witch or an innocent victim of circumstances.

"Tell me, Mistress Comstock. If Lucy Milborne got it into her head that some one person was responsible for the ills that have befallen her, would she be the sort to attempt to avenge herself upon him?"

"I do much doubt it. Weeping and wailing, not action, that was her way. Now, tell me about your mother."

When he was satisfied that there was no more Mistress Comstock could tell him about the former nun, Nick obliged as best he could. In truth, he knew little more about his mother's early days in London than he did of Lucy Milborne's life. As the wife of Bevis Baldwin, she'd acquired a good business sense and she was careful of money, but he did not think those facts would interest her old acquaintance. He related the essentials—her marriage to his father, the ventures both husband and son engaged in, the property in London and Northamptonshire and Kent. When he stopped speaking, Mistress Comstock regarded him in silence for a long moment.

"Good for her," she said at last. "Got what she wanted."

"And what was that?"

"Wealth. Respectability. Pity she did not see fit to share."

"What do you mean?"

"Well, you cannot deny that she left the rest of her family here to die in poverty."

There must be some mistake, Nick thought. He was certain his mother had told him, when he was just a lad, that she had no kin living.

Mistress Comstock, having decided to speak, could not be stopped. In considerable detail, she described the conditions under which Nick's grandparents and aunts, people he'd never known, had lived and died. The life his mother had lived until she was fifteen years old.

"Falling to ruin, next thing to a hovel," Mistress Comstock said of the family house. "Winifred slept in the garret, where the roof was in such disrepair that snow and rain came in on her and her sisters in the night. Still, 'twas a great surprise to folk hereabout when she ran away to London. I was already in Canterbury by then, but my kinfolk were happy to provide the details. She had a great blazing row with her father when she told him what she meant to do, and the next day she was gone. He warned her she'd end a whore, you see, if she went there all on her own. When he never heard from her again, everyone supposed she had."

With these remarkable revelations still reverberating inside his head, Nick bade Mistress Comstock farewell and left Croydon. If what she'd told him was true, his mother was not the woman he'd thought she was. The

Winifred Marley Mistress Comstock had described had put her own comfort, her own concerns, above everything and everyone else. That she'd not reconciled with her father he could understand, but how could she not have tried to help her sisters?

Worse, she had lied to him, her own son, about her family. His family.

Had she lied about other matters, as well?

She wanted Susanna out of his life. Hated her, in fact. He'd not wanted to admit that to himself but the truth was forced upon him now. That his mother had met with Chediok Norden boded ill. Had she lied about what transpired at their meeting? 'Twas all too possible.

She'd let Nick make the journey to Croydon, knowing he might uncover information about her past. There was only one reason he could think of for her to have taken such a risk. She'd wanted him out of the way so she could get at Susanna. He could not guess what she had planned, but if Norden was involved, he feared for Susanna's safety.

Once again, Nick rode hard, throughout the rest of the day and into the evening, through Keston and Halstead and Otford and Wrotham and Larkfield. He had but one goal—to get back to Susanna as quickly as he could.

36

Get rid of it," Jennet advised.

Susanna knew she was right. The vial she'd found in her capcase had not been put there by a benevolent soul. But if someone was determined to brand her a witch, they could make as much of discovering the infusion she took daily, a healthful blend of St. John's wort and ginger root.

"This proves nothing against me," she said to Jennet.

"It proves someone seeks to cause you trouble."

"Aye. It does that."

"Who left this here? What man dared come into your chamber while we were gone and—"

"Not a man. Winifred Baldwin."

Susanna wondered when she had managed it. With Lucy so ill, Susanna and Jennet had remained at the gaol most of the previous afternoon and evening. Since fresh herbs had been available in the marketplace, Susanna had not needed her capcase, and this morning she'd forgotten to take her tonic because she'd been so anxious to contact Hugo before he left The Ship for the day.

That had been a wasted effort. Once again, he had already departed by the time she got there. And Mildred Edgecumbe, too, had been missing. It was astonishing how completely folk could disappear in a town so much smaller than London. Crowds had already begun to gather for the Assizes. Trials began on Thursday, and that was market day, as well. She supposed it was possible there was nothing mysterious in losing track of two visitors to the place at such a time.

Especially if both were trying to avoid her.

Unable to pursue her investigation in that direction, Susanna and Jennet had returned to the gaol, where Lucy was now recovering rapidly. They'd arrived back at the Queen's Arms only a few minutes earlier.

"If you will not dispose of it, I will." Jennet seized the vial and flung it into the cold hearth. The glass container shattered, spewing a viscous green liquid across the stones. A pungent and unpleasant smell filled the room.

"Well done, Jennet."

But the act could not erase Susanna's knowledge that someone had planted the vial in her belongings or answer the question of why this had been done. On reflection, she did not believe Nick's mother intended to renounce her as a witch. To do so, she would have to reveal herself to the authorities and testify in court. If it came to that, she'd have no prayer of hiding what she'd done from her son.

An involuntary shudder racked Susanna. Perhaps that no longer mattered to the woman. Did Winifred Baldwin hate her that much? So much that she was willing to risk the loss of her son's love to destroy his mistress?

Nick had not yet returned to Maidstone, but perhaps the vial had been put there for him to find when he did. If so, Winifred had misjudged the strength of their feelings for each other. Susanna felt certain she knew how Nick would react. Even if she did not share her suspicions with him, he'd leave no stone unturned until he discovered who had sought to blacken her name. The trail would lead him straight back to Winifred, driving a wedge between mother and son.

Aware that Jennet was watching her, concern and confusion upon her face, Susanna shook off her unease. It was futile to engage in further speculation. Whatever Mistress Baldwin's plan had been, Jennet had most likely foiled it by destroying the vial.

And they had more important things to worry about. The assize clerks were already in town, arriving ahead of the judges to bring their records and a supply of stationery. The justices themselves would appear in Maidstone on the morrow. They'd come toward evening and open the first session early the following morning.

Susanna picked up the list Jennet had compiled at Mill Hall. "If only Nick would return. Or word would come from Canterbury. I have too many theories and no facts." She glanced at the first name. "I cannot care for Hugo Garrard but neither can I see how he profits from deaths past or deaths to come."

"Mildred Edgecumbe is more likely to be behind all that has happened." Jennet covered the bits of broken glass with kindling and dusted her hands on the sides of her apron. "She profits."

"Aye." A widow's position had great advantages over that of a wife. And Mildred had long disliked Lucy Milborne. But was jealousy of a woman Clement Edgecumbe had loved long ago reason enough to commit two murders and place the blame on two innocent women?

"Mistress Edgecumbe could be a witch."

"She is not a witch. No one we have met is a witch." Susanna had strong doubts that anyone possessed the supernatural powers attributed to witches, and yet she was loath to insist witches could not exist. Much that had no explanation did happen. She compromised by refusing to blame every odd event on curses and spells.

"Mistress Damascin, then. What of her?" Jennet peered at the list over Susanna's shoulder. "I warrant she is no innocent miss."

"Being wanton, if she *is* wanton, does not make her a murderess." Kennison's claims were suspect by virtue of his drunken state and obvious resentment against Hugo. Such a one could say anything when he was in his cups.

"Lucy," Susanna continued, reading the next name on the list. "That she was once a nun seems to be the only mark against her. She may have resented Clement's gain at the church's loss and refused to marry him because of it, but there has to have been more reason than that for her to have killed him. She'd have acted years ago if that was the cause. Constance speaks of their quarrels as an ongoing source of enjoyment to Lucy. Why would she put an end to her favorite pastime? And there is nothing in Lucy's past to explain Marsh's murder."

"Unless he found out she'd killed Master Edgecumbe and threatened to expose her."

Because Jennet might be correct, Susanna made a note next to Lucy's name and went on to Constance. "Peter Marsh," she said aloud. "Who was he? What did he want? Was there a connection between his courtship of Damascin and his subsequent interest in Constance? Or was he simply the sort of man who tried to seduce every woman he met?"

"Constance might be lying. She could have killed Marsh to keep any other woman from having him."

"But why kill Clement? Oh, I know Lucy is the one accused in his death, but the crimes are linked. They must be."

"Mayhap Constance meant to kill Damascin and made a mistake."

"You are too good at playing devil's advocate," Susanna complained. "What reason can you think of then, to say Norden is our murderer?"

Jennet chewed on her lower lip as she pondered. "He once worked at Edgecumbe Manor and thought himself in love with Mistress Damascin. Mayhap he still cares for her. Mayhap he believes that by writing his pamphlet he will earn fame and fortune and the hand of the fair maiden."

"If he does, he will be disappointed. But how does that make him our murderer? It would be Hugo he'd have to kill to get Damascin."

"But Norden is the one most likely to have known what was in the earlier pamphlet. Mayhap it gave him the idea to create a subject for his own."

"A devious plot, Jennet. Too devious."

"He is a devious fellow. Master Baldwin's man, Simon, told me that Master Norden paid a call on Mistress Baldwin."

"When?"

"Early yesterday morning."

Susanna was uncertain how to interpret this information, but she did not like the sound of it. Norden clearly thought she was a witch. Was that why he had sought out Winifred? Or had she sent for him? Suddenly, she was very glad Jennet had broken the vial.

"What of Arthur Kennison?" Jennet asked.

Susanna drew a line through his name. It felt good to be able to eliminate someone from the list of suspects. She was considering also crossing off Sir Adrian when someone knocked at her chamber door.

Nick did not wait to be invited in. Dust-covered and travel-stained, his exhaustion plain on his beloved face, he burst into the room. "Praise God," he whispered when his eyes found her. An instant later, she was in his arms.

"I am very glad to see you, too," she told him long moments later.

"I feared for your safety. Mine own mother may be involved in some foul scheme with Chediok Norden."

Susanna did not tell him about the vial. "I've not seen your mother since she learned of your plans to travel to Hamburg. Indeed, no one from your household has come near us."

"I sent Toby with a letter before I left. Do you mean to say you did not receive it."

At the negative shake of her head, Nick scowled, warming Susanna's heart. "Toby would not disobey you, Nick. There must be another explanation."

"Oh, yes. Of that I am certain. My mother." He told her then what he knew of Norden's meeting with Winifred and also all he had learned about her in Sussex.

"She practices petty mischief attempting to put us in disfavor with each other."

"She'll not succeed."

"No."

"But Norden . . . I cannot like his role in this."

"Perhaps your mother told you the truth about him. That he sought her out to learn more about me, her neighbor. Certes, if they meant to act in your absence, he has missed his cue. I am here, safe, and no one has troubled me." Over Nick's shoulder she shot Jennet a warning glance.

"You are right. My fears seem to be proven groundless. And here I am, back well before anyone would expect my return."

"And starved, no doubt, for food and for news." Sending Jennet for refreshments, she gave him an account of her activities during the time he had been gone. She was frowning when she was done. "In truth, I have made no progress at all."

"But you have," he protested, reaching for a wedge of the cheese Jennet had just brought in. "Everything you learn has a place in the whole. When you have enough pieces, the pattern will become evident."

"Then let us add the pieces you've discovered. Did you learn anything about Lucy in Croydon?"

Over wine and bread and more cheese, Nick told Susanna and Jennet what Mistress Comstock had told him. "In spite of her opinion, it seems to me that a tendency toward weeping and wailing might easily turn into madness, even violence."

"You think Lucy could be guilty?"

"Not of witchcraft, perhaps, but of poisoning those two men. Yes, I do think it possible."

"And yet, I have seen no sign she is the sort to become easily distraught, or to act from high emotion. The fervor she felt in her youth seems to have been tempered by age, not increased by it." She wondered if the same could be said of Winifred Baldwin.

"You know her better than I," Nick conceded, "but I am too tired to think of any other explanation."

Motioning for Jennet to leave them alone, Susanna went to him and wrapped her arms around his waist. "Come to bed then," she invited. "Let us leave off thinking altogether until morning."

37

WEDNESDAY, JULY 9, 1567

Margery, the tiring maid Mistress Edgecumbe and her daughter had brought with them to Maidstone, did not have enough experience at skulking to spy on Lady Appleton's entourage without being seen. She should have been able to fade into the background with ease. There was nothing about her physical appearance to make her stand out in the early-morning bustle at the Queen's Arms, but she was so ill at ease, so nervous of being discovered, that her fidgeting drew all eyes to her. More amused than outraged, Jennet bided her time, then accosted the woman when she abruptly abandoned the premises of the hostelry and fled into the innyard.

"Why not just ask what you want to know?" she inquired. "Lady Appleton has nothing to hide." Master Baldwin had left before dawn so as not to taint her reputation.

"Nor does my mistress," Margery declared, but the slide of her eyes away from Jennet's intense gaze betrayed her.

"Mildred Edgecumbe has the best motive of anyone for doing away with her husband, and her own daugh-

ter told us how she did much dislike Peter Marsh."
'Twould be wonderful to solve both murders, Jennet
thought, to impress Lady Appleton with her sleuthing
skills. "Why, I'll wager she even caused the bucking
tub to be upset on my mistress the day we visited Edgecumbe Manor."

"Oh, no, Jennet!" Margery protested. "That was
Mistress Damascin's fault."

Unable to believe her ears, Jennet gripped Margery's
arm tight enough to elicit a gasp of pain. "What did
you say?"

"Mistress Damascin upset the tub."

"That is not possible. She was in the house. And
why would she do such a thing?"

" 'Twas not deliberate. Oh, you must not think
that." Margery looked about to burst into tears.

Calming herself with an effort, Jennet drew the
other woman into the shelter of the inn's stable. They
were attracting too much attention standing in the
open. "Tell me what did happen, then. How could
Mistress Damascin have tipped over the bucking tub
without my noticing she had returned to the yard?"

Sulking a bit, Margery cast a baleful look in Jennet's
direction before she answered. "I told you before that
Mistress Damascin likes to dress up."

The widow's weeds at the church. Jennet frowned.
"Do you mean to tell me your mistress went back into
the house, disguised herself as a servant, and returned
to tip boiling water onto my mistress?"

"She never done it on purpose."

Damascin in disguise. Jennet shook her head to clear
it. She tried to envision the scene at Edgecumbe Manor.
In a plain kirtle and with her crown of fair hair covered
by a servant's wimple, perhaps even a straw hat—the
day had been hot and sunny—her presence might have
gone unremarked among the other women.

"Why would she do such a thing? Dress up, I mean."

Margery looked relieved that Jennet seemed to accept her word that the spill of water had been an accident. "Oh, that is simple enough to explain. She disguised herself as a servant for the fun of it. 'Tis something she has done before and she always rewards us well for keeping her secrets."

Margery held up her hands to show Jennet a fine pair of gloves with embroidery on the cuffs. They were almost new and scarce worn, although Jennet could not help but notice there was a small burn on one finger. The result, no doubt, of a rich young woman's carelessness. Still, such castoffs were not to be sneered at.

"Your mistress is indeed generous."

"That day, Mistress Damascin comed out to join us in our work whilst you and your mistress were busy with Mistress Edgecumbe. She ain't the lazy creature her mother would make of her. She growed tired of not being allowed to try new things. Such treatment just makes her try hard not to be catched."

Such treatment, Jennet thought, would not make most young women so rebellious. It must be passing sweet to be pampered. In spite of Margery's spirited defense, Jennet could not bring herself to think kindly of Damascin Edgecumbe. That she had disguised herself as a servant meant only that she was deceitful as well as clever.

"She wanted to help with the water," Margery continued, "but she is not as well muscled as a laundress must be. The cauldron was too heavy for her. 'Twas just ill luck that we stumbled with it and overset the bucking tub at the very moment your mistress passed by on the other side."

It could have been an accident, Jennet supposed. After all, what reason would Damascin have had to harm Lady Appleton? She'd not even known why they were at Edgecumbe Manor that day—unless she'd been near enough to overhear what Lady Appleton had said to her mother.

"Dresses up often, does she?" Jennet asked Margery.

"Oh, aye." She giggled. "You'd not believe some of the things she wears."

"But if she is innocent in all this, why did she send you to spy on Lady Appleton? What does it matter to her what my mistress does?"

To Jennet's surprise, this question produced another giggle. "It was not Mistress Damascin sent me. 'Twas her mother."

38

Susanna listened to Jennet's account of her conversation with Margery with mild amusement but little concern.

"While you were out, Jennet, a letter at last arrived from Canterbury. What Master Calthorpe has learned about Lucy's past may mean we need not concern ourselves further with Mildred or Damascin."

"He discovered something?"

"Indeed, he did. A motive for all that has transpired." She glanced at the missive. "The solution is both simple and obvious, now that one significant fact has come to light."

"What is it? What did you find out?" Jennet's eagerness made her a most appreciative audience.

"Lucy Milborne is the rightful owner of Mill Hall, not Hugo Garrard. It came to her at her brother's death. Do you remember, Jennet? Lucy told us there was a quarrel between male cousins when he died. She may not realize that she is an heiress. It is possible that she was somehow tricked out of her birthright."

"Mayhap what Master Baldwin learned explains her confusion. Did he not say her state of mind grew perilous when the nunnery was closed?"

"Excellent, Jennet. That may be the answer. We will go to the gaol and talk to Lucy. I think we will discover that she was indeed defrauded of her inheritance, by Hugo's father and then by Hugo."

"You mean Master Garrard is—?"

"The murderer." It made perfect sense to her. "If Clement Edgecumbe knew Lucy should have inherited, because of his interest in marrying her when her father was still alive, the matter would have come up when Hugo proposed to marry Damascin. Hugo must have feared the truth would come out and he'd lose not only Damascin but Mill Hall, as well. That gave him a powerful reason to kill Edgecumbe. The same motive applies to Marsh's death. He was Hugo's clerk before Adrian Ridley came. What more likely than that he knew too much of his master's affairs and became suspicious when Clement died? Then he had to be silenced, too. Blaming Lucy may not have been Hugo's original plan, but he'd have been passing quick to think of it once he decided to commit the second murder."

"Proving any of this will be difficult."

Susanna dismissed Jennet's pessimism with an airy wave of her hand, pleased to discover that it no longer surprised her with pain when she made a sudden move.

An hour later, Susanna met with Constance and Lucy in their cell. For a change, she was their only visitor. Sir Adrian was nowhere to be seen, and Susanna had sent Jennet to Nick's house to apprise him of this newest development.

He had left her to go home hours earlier, with great reluctance, to have a serious talk with his mother.

Lucy, much recovered but still weak, listened to Susanna's reasoning without interrupting, but her occasional nod seemed to indicate agreement.

"Did you know you could inherit after your brothers died, if they had no children?"

"Aye. I did. But by entering the nunnery, I relinquished that right."

"You regained it with the dissolution."

Lucy frowned. "If I was told that, it was lost in the long period when my mind was . . . disturbed. I have only a few, muddled memories of the period right after my father brought me home."

"Your relatives took advantage of that." Susanna was convinced that Hugo was behind Lucy's troubles.

"I can scarce believe it," Constance said. "I trusted Hugo to—oh!"

"What is it, Constance?"

"The letter!"

"What letter?"

"I wrote a letter to you when I was arrested, asking for your help. I gave it to Hugo to send to Leigh Abbey."

"I never received any letter, Constance."

Constance looked stunned by this news. "But if you did not receive it, why did you offer to help us? I assumed you'd gotten the letter and were not in any hurry to offer assistance, but I did not mention how long you took to respond because, after all, you did come forward in the end."

"I came because you were unjustly accused," Susanna told her. "It was by chance that I was in Maidstone and heard of the case."

After a few minutes' thought, Constance sighed. "That Hugo should have done this makes a terrible kind of sense. Even Peter Marsh's sudden interest in me can be explained by this new information. He must have fixed his attention to me because he knew I was Lucy's heiress. But do you have any evidence that can convince the justices we are innocent?"

"I have speculation, not proof and yet, with luck, that will be enough to postpone the trial. When the justices arrive in Maidstone later today, I will go to them and present your case in private."

"How can you——?"

"There are names I can drop in order to gain access to these men." With what she'd learned this morning, Susanna felt confident they would give her a fair hearing.

39

Jennet was on her way back to the Queen's Arms from Master Baldwin's house when she heard that the justices had been sighted just outside of Maidstone. Thinking this sufficient excuse for a detour, she went to the gaol, intending to inform her mistress of their impending arrival.

To her surprise, there was someone just outside the door of the cell. He had an ear to the door, blatantly eavesdropping on the conversation within. A servant lad, by the look of his clothing, he was not anyone she recognized.

"Hey, you!" Jennet shouted.

The boy ran. Jennet followed, emerging into the bright sunlight barely in time to see the direction he took. Hoisting up her skirts, she sped after him, unsurprised when he turned down the side street that led to The Ship.

Panting, her side on fire from a stitch, Jennet reached the inn only moments after the lad disappeared within. What now? Margery, she decided. She would find Margery and ask about servant lads in the Edgecumbes' employ.

But Margery, so the inn's chamberlain informed her, had gone out, as had Mistress Edgecumbe.

"And her daughter?"

He shrugged. "I did not notice."

With the justices coming, the atmosphere of a fair pervaded Maidstone. Most folk were out and about, coming and going.

"Did a lad run in here just ahead of me?"

"Oh, aye. I passed him just now on the stair. Like as not, he went into the chamber Mistress Edgecumbe and her daughter share."

Jennet felt no trepidation about approaching the room the chamberlain had indicated was Mildred Edgecumbe's. Mistress Edgecumbe was not there, only a boy, and Jennet was an old hand at dealing with servant lads.

Without pausing to wonder if she was acting wisely, she opened the door and stepped into the room.

40

Susanna read through the pages of the deposition she had just finished writing, well satisfied with the result. She had marshaled all the facts in a clear and rational manner. Although she intended to plead her case before the justices in person, documentation was never amiss. Confident that she would be able to keep her promise to Lucy and Constance and obtain a postponement of their trial, she folded the newly inscribed pages around Master Calthorpe's letter.

In this case, postponement might well be as good as an acquittal. Susanna intended to use every bit of influence she could muster, and a few judicious bribes, as well, to obtain the prisoners' release. She would also offer sureties for their return in six months, but with any luck, by the time the Assizes met again, this furor over witches would have died down. Even if Mildred Edgecumbe could not be persuaded to withdraw her charges, with that much time they could find more proof that poison, not witchcraft, had killed Clement Edgecumbe and Peter Marsh. Now that they had uncovered Hugo Garrard's motive, evidence of his guilt would surely follow.

Standing, Susanna stretched her arms high above her head and flexed her cramped fingers. She left the table to wander idly about the chamber, and not for the first time wondered where Jennet had gotten to. Susanna had expected her friend to be waiting for her here at the Queen's Arms. Jennet had left the inn hours earlier to deliver a message to Nick. Neither Fulke nor Lionel had seen her since.

Although Susanna was puzzled by Jennet's continued absence, she was not particularly worried. There were a great many places Jennet could be, including Nick's house. Yes, Susanna decided. That must be it. Jennet knew Nick planned to return to the inn. Indeed, he should be arriving at any moment. No doubt Jennet had waited, intending to accompany him.

That thought brought a frown to Susanna's face. The only reason she could think of for Jennet to spend time in Nick's company was in order to talk about her, Susanna. An uneasy truce had existed between them since Susanna had taken up residence at the Queen's Arms, but she did not expect it to last. Jennet was, in her own way, as opposed to Susanna's involvement with Nick as Nick's mother was.

It was pure chance that brought Susanna, pacing, close to her door at the moment a small object was shoved through the gap beneath it. She picked up what appeared to be a thin packet with one hand and lifted the latch with the other, stepping out of the chamber in time to catch sight of a boy just reaching the top of the stair. A moment later, he'd disappeared from view.

He'd left behind a piece of paper folded around a lock of Jennet's hair. The accompanying note was brief but terrifying.

Jennet—loyal, courageous Jennet—was being held prisoner. If Susanna wanted to see her again alive, she was to abandon her championship of Lucy and Constance and stay away from the justices.

Susanna had moved toward the window, where the light was better, as she read. When she lifted her gaze from the paper, she found herself staring blindly down into the innyard. Abruptly, her vision sharpened. The boy she'd just seen outside her door was there, crossing the open space between inn and stable and headed straight for the High Street.

Her only thought to catch up with that boy and make him tell her who had given him the message to bring to her, Susanna rushed out of her chamber. She dared not risk losing sight of her quarry by taking the time to fetch Lionel or Fulke to help her.

The crowds that delayed the boy's escape also frustrated Susanna's pursuit. All along Maidstone's High Street, she had to force her way through a milling throng. The justices were about to arrive.

Pandemonium reigned. Susanna could scarce hear herself think for the cacophony of sound—bells, music by the town waits, whistles and huzzahs at the first glimpse of the colorful cavalcade. Pikemen specially clothed for the occasion in bright new livery came first, walking ahead of the riders. The assize judges, one a justice of the Queen's Bench and the other a newly appointed serjeant-at-law, had been met a few miles outside of town by the county sheriff, the members of the corporation that governed Maidstone, and sundry representatives of the local gentry.

Susanna's original plan had been to join this very procession, following it to the inn in which the judges would lodge. There, by tradition, they received county gentlemen and heard their opinions on local matters. Now she wished these same men to perdition, for they impeded her progress.

Up ahead, she saw the boy break free of the crowd. He was heading, she realized, toward The Ship. Increasing her own efforts, she followed. She could not catch him. Even without the obstacles in her path, he had the advantage of youth and speed. But she was close enough behind to see where he went. When a chamber door slammed shut on the upper floor of The Ship, she was just cresting the stairwell. She saw which room he'd gone into.

Cautiously Susanna approached the closed door. She did not know whose chamber this was but thought it likely Hugo Garrard was within. She knew she should go back to the Queen's Arms for help but her concern for Jennet had her pressing her ear against the wooden portal.

She heard nothing. No voices. No sound whatsoever.

It would take too long to go back to the Queen's Arms. Were there men below, in The Ship's common room? Would they help her apprehend the boy who'd entered this room? No, she decided. They did not know her, and she would be asking them to invade the privacy of a paying guest.

She had no choice. She could not dawdle here all day. Besides, with Fulke and Lionel beside her, she'd have a better chance of convincing whoever they found within to cooperate. She should have guessed the boy would come here, she berated herself. She should have stopped to collect her henchmen en route.

Still cursing her lack of foresight, Susanna backed away from the chamber. Behind her, another door opened. She whirled around just as Hugo Garrard stepped out.

He swore when he caught sight of her.

She thought about running, but he blocked her escape route.

Trapped, Susanna gave the first excuse that popped into her mind. "I had hoped to speak to Mildred Edgecumbe, but it appears she has gone out." She moved toward him, hoping he would let her pass.

Hugo's hand shot out to stop her, closing around her forearm with bruising force. "It will be better, I do think, if you join your friend."

The moment he shoved open the door to the chamber, Susanna saw Jennet. She was lying on the floor, a trickle of blood staining her white cap. Breaking free of Hugo's grip, Susanna rushed to her friend's side. As she knelt, she realized that Jennet's hands and feet were bound.

"Leave her be," a woman's voice commanded. "So far she has suffered nothing more serious than a blow to the head with a stout stick."

Susanna's hasty survey of the damage was sufficient to reassure her that this was true. She could not like the fact that Jennet was unconscious, but her breathing was regular and her color good.

Rising slowly, Susanna turned. Hugo had gone to stand by the window. Mildred Edgecumbe was nowhere in sight. It had been Damascin who'd issued the command.

"So," Susanna murmured, "you are the instigator of it all."

"Why so amazed, Lady Appleton? I would think you'd be the first to admit that a woman can be clever and resourceful."

Certes, she had the right of it. Too late, Susanna recognized the simple truth that Damascin, as well as Hugo, stood to gain by the deaths of Edgecumbe, Marsh, Lucy, and Constance.

"I do not discount the murderous capabilities of females, Damascin. Indeed, I had thought that perhaps your mother—"

Damascin's high-pitched laugh cut short the remark. "Mother had no part in this." Contempt laced her voice. A sneer made otherwise pretty features ugly.

"Your Margery told Jennet 'twas Mildred Edgecumbe sent her to spy on us."

"And so she did, after I convinced her that she should."

"Where is your mother?" Had they done away with her, too?

"Gone to watch the procession. She will not trouble us. Nor help you, Lady Appleton. You need not think it."

"I rely upon no one but myself" Susanna told her.

She looked around for the boy she had followed. The only sign of him was a heap of discarded garments scattered across the bed. In her head, Susanna heard Jennet's voice, quoting Margery: *Likes to dress up, does Mistress Damascin.*

"Courtesy of the stable boy at Edgecumbe Manor?" Susanna asked, indicating the disguise.

"Make yourself useful, Lady Appleton. Finish lacing me up." Damascin had resumed her own clothing but had not been able to fasten the back of her bodice or properly attach her sleeves.

Susanna obliged her, though she found the task distasteful. She entertained, briefly, a fantasy of using the young woman's own points to strangle her. She deserved no better fate after all she'd done.

Unfortunately, with Hugo close at hand, any such attempt would be doomed to failure. Better to cooperate, Susanna decided. She would bide her time until she could devise a foolproof plan to remove both herself and Jennet from the clutches of this murderous couple.

"We must change our plans," Hugo said. "Again. I like this not."

Damascin ignored him. "You were unwise to take matters into your own hands, Lady Appleton. Now, what are we to do with you?"

"You could release us.

"I do not think so."

"Was this your plan from the first?"

"Yes," Damascin boasted.

"To kill your own father?"

"Aye. Why not? He meant to ruin all. He tried to stop me marrying Hugo when he realized that Hugo was not the true owner of Mill Hall."

"You could have found other prospective husbands, some richer, mayhap, than Hugo Garrard."

"None would have been so well suited to my needs."

"Clement Edgecumbe would have ruined me," Hugo asserted, moving up beside Damascin to wrap an arm around that young woman's shoulders. "Ruined us. He threatened to enlighten Lucy as to the true state of affairs. We could not allow that."

"Lucy should have been forced to sign away her rights when she left the nunnery." Scorn laced Damascin's reproach.

"An oversight on my father's part. He thought it unnecessary since he'd convinced her she had no property, that he was the heir to it all."

"So," Susanna said, "Clement Edgecumbe was the only one who suspected that Lucy was in line to inherit ahead of your father."

Hugo nodded. "Once he'd sought to marry Lucy, before she became a nun. Lucy was not the only heir back then, but her father had made a will to say that Lucy would inherit should her brothers die childless. Clement remembered that will when I asked to marry Damascin. He inquired about it and for some reason did not accept my word that the document was invalid." Hugo looked offended, but Damascin's face wore a sneer that did not augur well for harmony in their marriage. "Thinking that Lucy might know naught of her father's disposition of the property, Clement voiced his intention to speak with her about it."

And that, Susanna thought sadly, had cost him his life.

"What need had Lucy for Mill Hall?" Hugo grumbled. "She never wanted it."

It was possible, Susanna thought, that Lucy did not care who owned Mill Hall, so long as she and Constance were provided for. But it was too late now to speculate on what might have been.

Shrugging off Hugo's arm, Damascin crossed the room to rummage in a capcase she'd stored beneath the bed. Susanna kept her eyes on Hugo. He was, except in the physical sense, the weaker of the two, but the very fact that both Hugo and Damascin were willing to answer her questions disturbed her. Doubtless they allowed themselves the luxury of boasting only because they meant to kill her. And Jennet.

Susanna had some hope they would be rescued. She had dropped the note about Jennet in her chamber at the Queen's Arms. Nick should already have arrived there and found it. Once he read it, knowing what he did about Hugo, he might well guess who had been behind Jennet's abduction. If he did, surely he'd come here. She had only to stall the conspirators until he arrived.

"Why did Peter Marsh have to die?" she asked.

"He was the one who started Father thinking." Damascin spit out the words, darting a venomous look at Hugo. "While he served as a clerk at Mill Hall, he saw some papers he should not have seen."

And after Clement's sudden death, Susanna speculated, Marsh had become suspicious.

"You need not look sympathetic, Lady Appleton. He deserved to die."

Damascin's scorn for her second victim seemed

greater than that she'd expressed toward her father. Mayhap because he'd once admired her?

"He tried to extort money from me for his silence and at the same time he went behind my back to court Constance, ugly hag that she is. He helped Lucy make a will and knew Constance was her heir. When he realized he could not have me, that I was to wed Hugo, he meant to thwart our plans by marrying her and claiming Mill Hall for himself."

"Could you not control him?" In a taunting voice, Susanna strove to drive a wedge between the conspirators. " 'Tis plain you give Hugo his orders."

This time Damascin's laugh sounded genuine. "Marsh was greedy. And a fool. He had to die."

A glance in Hugo's direction showed Susanna new tension in his shoulders. He was watching Damascin with wary eyes and tugging with nervous fingers at his beard.

"Fine behavior for a man who wants to be appointed a justice of the peace!"

Startled, Hugo shifted his attention to Susanna. "I will have that honor, and others, too. All who stand in my way will be dealt with."

"Poor fool." She pretended to hold him in contempt, though her overriding emotion was pity. "Damascin will marry you. No doubt of that. But will you long survive afterward? You have shown a grievous lack of judgment, Master Garrard, that bodes ill for your advancement in county government. 'Twill only compound your error to murder me. If you had no hand in poisoning those two men, and I warrant you did not, the law might be inclined to leniency. Let Damascin pay for what she has done. Bring her to justice. Free those two innocent women. Redeem yourself."

A low-throated growl issued from Damascin's throat. "He will do what I say. They all do what I say."

"Not Peter Marsh." As soon as the words were out, Susanna wished she'd kept her opinion to herself. The young woman glaring at her was dangerous. Unpredictable. Her eyes were overbright and her face was flushed, both signs of intense emotion . . . or overuse of some stimulating herb.

"Save your arguments, Lady Appleton," Hugo said. "Damascin and I understand each other."

"But you have no hope of success now. I am not the only one who knows Lucy is the rightful owner of Mill Hall."

"Liar!" Damascin's face contorted. She stepped close to slap Susanna hard across the face. Susanna's head snapped back. She tasted blood and her cheek stung from the force of the blow.

Total silence fell inside the chamber. They could hear faint echoes of the celebration going on in the town but no one spoke for a long moment. Then Hugo whispered a question. "What if she is telling the truth?"

"It does not matter," Damascin insisted. "I have worked it all out. Constance may be Lucy's heir, but you are heir to all Constance possesses when she dies. As for Lady Appleton, she will be as silent as I wished her to be. She will disappear, along with her servant." She gestured toward Jennet's motionless form.

Had Jennet's position shifted? Susanna thought it had and hoped she was correct. If Jennet was conscious and listening, their chances of survival were much improved.

"Once we spirit them away from here," Damascin continued, "we will spread more rumors, stories to make people think Lady Appleton is a witch, too, and that she used magic to escape the law. When evidence is found in her chamber at the Queen's Arms, proving she dabbled in spells and sorcery, no one will doubt this reasoning. Seize her, Hugo."

Before Susanna could elude him, Hugo pinned her arms behind her back. Damascin unstoppered a glass vial, doubtless the object she'd retrieved from her cap-case. She advanced toward her intended victim, her face a mask of malevolence.

Susanna recognized the contents of the vial, both by smell and taste. She fought not to swallow, but it was no use. Despite her best efforts to keep her lips tightly sealed, enough dribbled into her mouth to accomplish Damascin's purpose.

Helpless, her senses reeling, Susanna collapsed against Hugo. Her last coherent thought gave her only small comfort: at least the vial had not contained bane-wort.

41

Nick scarce heard the church bells sound to announce the arrival of the assize judges. His mind was still struggling to assimilate the shocks of the morning.

Had he ever truly known his own mother?

That she'd lied to him had been bad enough, but in some ways he almost wished she'd continued to lie when he'd confronted her, that she'd invented some new story. Anything would have been better than the truth.

She'd abandoned her family completely after she left Croydon, although she'd known full well how destitute her sisters were. When she might have helped them, she did not make the slightest effort on their behalf not even to discover if they were still alive. She'd made no apologies for that, either. According to her, sisters and father alike had turned their backs on her, turned her out. Insulted her. She owed them nothing but contempt.

That she'd have felt the sting of her father's damning prophecies so strongly confused Nick further. By her own confession, once in London, Winifred Marley *had* turned whore to keep body and soul together.

Oh, she had not gone to work in a brothel. Nick supposed he should be grateful for small favors. What she'd admitted to, angry rather than tearful at being found out, was that she'd become the assistant to a third-rate astrologer. And his mistress.

She'd met Bevis Baldwin, Nick's father, when he'd visited that astrologer, as many merchants did, to ask the most propitious time to start a new venture. The stars had advised him to purchase shares in a certain shipping venture. Winifred had suggested, after one look at him, or mayhap at his fat purse, that he enter another sort of venture with her. When he'd hesitated, she'd purchased a love charm—not a love potion, she'd been quick to assure him, as if that distinction made any great difference—and within a month they were married. She'd become respectable again.

Had his father ever known about the love charm? He had, it seemed, been able to accept that his new wife did not come to him a virgin. They had always appeared, at least to their only son, to have a loving relationship, one based on affection and on mutual trust. Nick had seen Bevis Baldwin look at his wife in a way that reminded him of the intensity of his own feelings for Susanna.

But as Nick paced the parlor, hours after the session with his mother had deteriorated into bitter words and recriminations and she'd fled to the isolation of her bedchamber in a temper, he wondered if he had really known either of his parents as well as he'd once thought.

Raking his fingers through his hair, Nick paused to stare at his own reflection in the windowpane. It was already past the hour he'd promised to meet Susanna at the Queen's Arms, but there was no help for it. He had other matters left to discuss with his mother. He would finish this now. If there were worse revelations ahead, he would deal with each as it came.

Nick climbed a flight of narrow stairs to his mother's chamber, the same chamber Susanna had used on the one night she'd spent under this roof. "Did my father know all?" he blurted when he found Winifred, composed and dry eyed, propped up against the pillows on the bed.

"Aye. He did."

Nick believed her. However their marriage had come about, Bevis Baldwin had loved his wife and Winifred had devoted herself to him and to the business and to their son. To him. Nick understood, although he deplored the fact, that even his mother's irrational dislike of Susanna stemmed from love, from a desire to do what she believed was best for him.

With a sigh, he sank down beside her. "In my travels abroad, I have seen poverty, poverty more deplorable than anything to be found in England. There were far worse things you might have done to stay alive. But I cannot help but wish you'd been able to reconcile with your family. I'd have liked to have known them." To have helped them, too.

"What's done is done. I do not have time enough left in my life for guilt or regrets."

"You do have time to correct a more recent . . . mistake."

Her gaze sharpened. "What mistake?"

"Chediok Norden. You lied to me about him, Mother."

"Nonsense." Even though she denied it, she could not hide the flash of fear in her eyes.

"This morning, before I talked to you, I sent Simon and Toby out to scour the town for Norden. They came back an hour ago to report that no one has seen him since Susanna encountered him in the common room at The Ship on the day I left Maidstone for Croydon."

When an expression of surprise flickered across her face, Nick's suspicions heightened. He forced himself to harden his heart against his mother. He had to find out the truth. The message Susanna had sent with Jennet seemed to indicate she'd found a way to save Lucy and Constance, but he could not quite shake off the sense that something else threatened Susanna herself.

"Charges of witchcraft are naught to trifle with, Mother."

"What mean you, Nick?"

"You must have heard someone arrive with a message earlier. Susanna has found out the truth. Hugo Garrard had good and sufficient reason to conspire to have his cousins blamed for the deaths of Clement Edgecumbe and Peter Marsh. It is only a matter of time now before we can prove that Constance Crane and Lucy Milborne had naught to do with it."

"They are not witches?"

"No." Unless someone else came forward to charge Lucy Milborne with doing harm through her attempts to heal, both women would eventually be set free.

His mother's frown deepened. "That's naught to do with me."

"Is it not? Tell me what Norden said to you, Mother. Everything. I know you lied to me about other matters. I can forgive you for that, but if you deceive me again . . ." He let his voice trail off leaving the threat unspoken.

Silence answered him.

"Did he accuse Susanna of witchcraft?"

"She's not the right match for you, Nick."

"I know you disapprove of Susanna. I even understand why. You need not concern yourself about my posterity, Mother. I mean to marry, in time, and there will be a child to inherit what you and Father built."

He spoke no less than the truth. Susanna was not yet past childbearing age. And there was always Rosamond.

The change in his mother was immediate. "Do you mean that, Nick?"

"Aye. I do."

"Then Lady Appleton did not bewitch you?"

"Is that what you thought? That she used a love charm?"

"I feared so, or a love potion, but I could find no proof of either."

"That is why you were searching my things at Whitethorn Manor?" Astonishment made his voice hitch.

His mother heaved a deep sigh and looked him straight in the eye. "When I did not find anything to incriminate her, I went to the local cunning woman and purchased a love potion. I meant for you to find it in her things, Nick. Nothing more. I thought you would realize then that she is not for you."

"There's irony!"

She looked bewildered.

"Father forgave you. Why should you think it so impossible that I would forgive Susanna?" Not that he'd have needed to. Susanna would have denied the love potion was hers and he'd have believed her.

"Can you forgive me, Nick?"

"For trying to protect me? Yes, Mother, I can. But this must stop now. You are not to interfere in my life again."

"There is more. I must make a clean breast of it. Norden saw me buy that love philtre. He followed me back here and threatened to have me arrested if I did not help him prove Lady Appleton a witch."

"What?" This was worse than he'd feared.

"Norden seemed certain that she was one and that she'd helped those two women in gaol to commit murder."

"How could you believe him?"

On the defensive again, only grudgingly admitting her own culpability, Nick's mother confessed the rest of it. Nick was still trying to make sense of Norden's mad scheme when they were interrupted by a vigorous pounding at the front door.

Amid great noise and confusion below stairs, Nick heard young Toby shout. "Master! Master! He's come here!" A moment later, breathless, the boy dashed into the bedchamber. " 'Tis the fellow you sent us to seek, Master Baldwin. Goodman Norden. He's demanding to speak with you."

Winifred's face lost all its color. "Send him away," she whispered.

"I am tempted to have him thrown in gaol for all the trouble he's caused," Nick said, "but such an action would only produce more difficulties." For both Winifred and Susanna.

Instead he descended to the lower level. Toby was at his side, but they left Winifred behind. Nick reached the small entryway in time to see Simon prevent an excessively tall young man with straw-colored hair from pushing past him into the main part of the house.

Norden.

But he had not come alone. He was accompanied by a plain-faced young woman Nick did not recognize, and by two young men who were most familiar to him—Fulke and Lionel.

"What means this uproar?" Nick demanded.

Everyone tried to answer at once. None of what they said made any sense, but when Lionel withdrew a folded sheet of inexpensive paper from the inner pocket of his jerkin, Nick seized it. It was the work of a moment to read the short message it contained. Several seconds more were necessary before he could fully comprehend what that message signified.

"Silence!" he bellowed. When they obeyed, he

rounded on the hapless Lionel. "Where did you get this?"

"In Lady Appleton's chamber at the inn. It had fallen to the floor. She's gone, Master Baldwin. We know not where."

"How long ago did she leave the Queen's Arms?"

Neither Fulke nor Lionel could answer him, but Nick thought he could piece together what had happened. "She's gone to look for Jennet," he muttered. Placing herself in danger. If he'd only met Susanna when he'd promised to, he'd have been there when she received this message.

"She's not at The Ship," Fulke blurted in his gruff terse way. "We went there when he told us what happened to him." He jerked his head at Norden. "No one was there by the time we arrived. Not Lady Appleton. Not Jennet. Not Master Garrard nor Mistress Edgecumbe nor Mistress Damascin."

"Where did you find him?" Nick indicated Norden.

Norden stuttered out his own answer. "I found them."

Nick took a closer look at the pamphlet writer. His face was uncommon pale, and from the smell of him he had recently been most horrible sick. The young woman clung to his arm not to support herself but to keep him upright.

Gentling his voice, Nick addressed her. "Who are you, girl?"

Bobbing a curtsey, she spoke softly, forcing him to strain to hear her words. "Margery, sir. Mistress Damascin's tiring maid."

"What is your part in this?"

"She rescued me." Norden's voice was steadier now, stronger, but he held himself carefully, as if he might have a cracked or broken rib. "I have been held prisoner for most of the last two days."

"Start at the beginning." Nick was impatient to go in search of Susanna, but if she was not at The Ship, where Hugo had been lodging, then he did not know where to begin. He hoped Norden's tale might give him a clue.

"I have been a great fool, Master Baldwin."

"I know of your intent to bring about Lady Appleton's arrest. And I know my mother saw no sign of you when she went to stand on the church porch."

Norden winced at his frigid tone. "After I encountered Lady Appleton in the common room at The Ship, I went to speak with Mistress Damascin. I had not seen her since I left Kent for London, though I'd tried to talk with her when I first came back. Mistress Edgecumbe turned me away." He paused to gather his thoughts. Margery, whether to encourage him or to comfort him Nick could not say, patted his arm.

"At first, I thought she was all I remembered. Sweet. Beautiful. I told her of the arrangements I had made with Mistress Baldwin and she did praise me mightily for my cleverness. Said I had become a formidable witch hunter. But when I explained that I was a pamphlet writer and that I intended to tell her father's sad story, she told me I must not, that 'twould be a disservice to her to call more attention to the case."

He looked so downcast that Nick might have taken pity on him if he had not been concerned about Susanna's safety. "Go on.

"I was certain I was right about Lady Appleton, sure she was a witch. And I believed the charges against Mistress Milborne and Mistress Crane because Mistress Damascin and her mother had made them." He sighed deeply. "I adored her when we were young. When I left Kent, determined to make my fortune in London, it was to impress her. I even decided to become a pamphlet writer because of Damascin Edgecumbe. She loved to read them, you see—tales of wonders and disasters and sensational trials."

Damascin? Nick had never met her, but what Norden seemed to be implying about her stunned him. She was behind this? A gently bred young woman?

"Are you saying Damascin Edgecumbe is the one who learned the details of the Chelmsford trials from such a source and conceived the scheme to defraud old Lucy of her land?"

Norden blinked at him in confusion. "Defraud?"

"Never mind. Go on with your story. How did you come to be made prisoner?"

Disillusionment showing in his slumped and defeated posture, Norden continued in a monotone. "She must have thought I knew more than I did. When I protested that I must write the true relation of these events, she accused me of attempting to extort money from her to keep my silence. Said I was as bad as Peter Marsh. It all burst upon me then, that she must have lied about Mistress Milborne and Mistress Crane. In print, you see, my account could be compared to the Chelmsford pamphlet. I backed away from her in horror, tried to flee, but it was too late."

"She struck him on the head with her father's old walking stick," Margery said.

"How do you know this, Margery? Did you help her?"

At Nick's accusation, Margery flushed. "I was watching. Hidden. I was curious, and Jennet said—"

Nick held up a hand to stop the flow of words. "Say no more. If you sought to emulate Jennet, I can guess the rest."

Without warning, Margery began to cry. "She catched Jennet because of me."

Between sobs, Margery confessed that she'd listened in on more than one conversation between Fulke and

Lionel in the common room at the Queen's Arms. She'd been the one to tell her mistress, before Norden confronted her, that Jennet was more to Susanna than a mere servant. Margery was no fool. Once she'd heard the content of the note they'd found in Susanna's room, she'd known it came from Damascin, that Damascin had realized, thanks to Margery, that Susanna could be controlled by threats against Jennet.

Nick could offer no comfort. She was right. Without the inside knowledge Margery had provided, Damascin would never have guessed that a member of the gentry would place the life of one of her retainers above that of a gentlewoman.

Norden tightened his grip on the girl's waist and continued with the story her confession had interrupted. "Unconscious, bound, and gagged, I was moved from Damascin's chamber to Hugo Garrard's. I overheard enough when I regained my senses to know they'd decided they must kill me in order to keep their secret. They meant to make it look like an accidental drowning. When Margery helped me escape, she saved my life."

"How is it you went first to the Queen's Arms and not to fetch a constable?"

Margery wiped her eyes. "We did not know then that Mistress Damascin had catched Jennet. We thought she'd be at the Queen's Arms. That she'd tell us what to do. Passing clever, Jennet is."

"I agreed with Margery's reasoning," Norden said. "And I assumed Lady Appleton would be there to advise us, too."

"Then we found the note," Lionel said, speaking for the first time. "When we heard what had befallen Goodman Norden, we went straight to The Ship, thinking they must be holding Jennet where they'd kept him, but we were too late. Everyone was gone."

A renewed sense of urgency gripped Nick. "We will return to The Ship now. There may be some clue you missed, something that will tell us where Susanna and Jennet have been taken."

He thought he could guess what had happened. When they'd discovered Norden had escaped, the murderers had panicked and fled. But why take Jennet, and presumedly Susanna, with them?

He did not care for the most obvious answer to that question.

It seemed to take eons to cross Maidstone. The streets were still crowded with spectators. Moreover, the second procession connected with the assizes had just begun. This time the justices were on their way to church, attended by the sheriff, his chaplain, and an extensive entourage.

Nick debated stopping them to ask for help, but explanations would take too much time. He hurried on, followed by his own retinue. Even his mother had insisted on coming along, having overheard Norden's tale from a listening post just out of sight on the stairs.

"Baldwin? What's amiss?" From his place among the local ministers, Adrian Ridley had noticed them. Now he broke ranks to trot alongside Nick. By the very make up of Nick's party, he could tell they were bent on some business related to Lucy and Constance's trial.

Without slowing his steps, Nick summarized what he now knew of the conspiracy and what he surmised about the danger to Susanna. To his surprise, Ridley did not need much convincing to accept the truth of the story. How much, Nick wondered, had Garrard already confessed to his private chaplain?

There was no sign of Susanna, Jennet, Hugo, or Damascin at the inn, but Mildred Edgecumbe had returned. She stared at Nick and the others as if they'd lost their minds.

"I have been out enjoying the festivities and have only just returned," she told them. "I know nothing of what my daughter might have done in my absence, but I do assure you that she is an innocent. A sweet young girl incapable—"

Nick interrupted the defense to explain to her, in a few blunt sentences, exactly what her sweet young daughter *was* capable of doing. Shocked, Mildred lost all power of speech. Sputtering incoherently, her face purple, she appeared to be on the verge of an apoplectic fit.

Winifred drew Mildred aside, attempting to calm her. She talked to her in quiet tones while Nick scoured the chamber for any clue Susanna might have left behind. He found nothing. No sign she had ever been there.

Damascin and Hugo had her. He was certain of it now. And he had to assume that they had taken her because they still believed they could get away with their crimes. They must think that by disposing of Susanna and Jennet they would eliminate all threat of exposure.

With horrible clarity he could imagine what they planned to do. They'd kill again, then return to Maidstone as if nothing had happened. Thinking Norden was the only one they had to worry about, they'd count on the authorities accepting Hugo's word, as a gentleman, against that of a former servant. No doubt they'd also assume they could persuade Mildred, the doting parent, to support whatever story they told.

They were wrong. Others knew the truth. When Damascin and Hugo showed their faces again, they would be arrested.

That would be small comfort if Susanna was dead. Nick had never felt so powerless.

A hand touched his arm.

"I warrant Hugo's taken them to the ship," his mother said.

"This is The Ship. Do you mean they are being held in another room, as Norden was?"

"Not The Ship, Nick. A ship. His ship. Mistress Edgecumbe says that Hugo Garrard arranged for a pinnace of thirty tons to anchor nearby, at Newhithe where the river is deep. What better place to drown someone and make it seem an accident?"

42

Pressed down by the weight of water and her own saturated clothing, Susanna struggled to rise, to breathe again the pure, sweet air she knew was somewhere above her. She could make no headway. In spite of her best efforts, she was being pulled under by the current, away from the surface, away from the sunlight.

Something bumped against her, clawing at her skirts, and when she turned to look she saw it was her father. She was too late to save him. He had drowned.

But as tears blurred her vision and she whimpered, the face of the corpse changed. It was no longer Sir Amyas Leigh, but Robert Appleton, Susanna's husband.

As from a great distance, she heard her own voice whisper. *But Robert was poisoned.* She knew then that she must be dreaming.

The nightmare had a familiar quality. Still trapped by it and yet somehow able to view it from afar, Susanna knew that this was the same dream she'd had so often in the past, the recurring vision that had haunted her until she'd at last seen undeniable proof that Robert had not died by drowning.

She came out of the sleeping nightmare into a waking one. She was not in the sea, but she was on it. She could see nothing through an impenetrable darkness but the smells were unmistakable—tar, the brine provisions were stored in, the vinegar used to scour ships between voyages. Through the pounding in her head, the ache of her limbs, and the churning of her stomach, she perceived that she was lying on a hard, wooden surface. A floor that moved. She was in the hold of a ship.

Panic struck, fast and overwhelming, pinning her in place. She struggled to bring her hands up and discovered they were bound. Not by hempen rope, but by something softer. Velvet? Her feet were tied, too, with strips of fabric strong enough to keep her immobile even as a sharp pain lanced her chest and her breathing became irregular. She was going to die. At that moment, she had not the slightest doubt of it.

Once again something bumped against her, jarring her, momentarily penetrating the mists of her fear. A voice croaked out a single word, as if the speaker had to force it through a parched throat.

"Madam?"

Jennet. Jennet was here with her. In spite of her ever-increasing anxiety, Susanna managed to regain a modicum of control. When she'd last seen Jennet, her friend had been unconscious and bound and lying on the floor of Damascin Edgecumbe's chamber at The Ship Inn.

The Ship to a ship. A delicious pun. Hysteria threatened, then receded as Jennet spoke again.

"Madam?"

Susanna's laugh was a hollow, humorless sound. How could she not be amused? After all they had been through together, all they must now face, it struck her as absurd that Jennet should continue to address her so formally, that she would never presume to call her mistress by her Christian name.

Although her body still rebelled, Susanna's mind

had regained a measure of its accustomed sharpness. She was able to assess their situation without a renewal of the overwhelming, mind-numbing panic she'd felt when she first revived. She sent a quick prayer of thanksgiving heavenward, along with a plea for continued strength of will. She was far from feeling her normal self but neither was she held in thrall by the symptoms of her affliction.

Susanna forced herself to take calm, even breaths. She needed to think clearly, to plan, to discover some way to get out of this situation alive.

She had not been poisoned. Even as Damascin had forced the liquid into her mouth, she'd recognized the strange, sickeningly sweet smell of mandrake juice. Brain thief some called it. Just inhaling it was enough to cause drowsiness, and the few drops Damascin had managed to make her swallow had rendered her senseless within minutes. At a guess, that much of the narcotic, which had also been responsible for those vivid dreams, had kept her deeply asleep for some three or four hours, long enough to smuggle her out of the inn and aboard this vessel.

What irony, Susanna thought, her mind becoming clearer by the minute. Had her captors only known, they'd have done better not to drug her. Without the potion Damascin had given her, she'd have been completely incapacitated by now. The mandrake had actually helped to soothe the worst of Susanna's fears.

Cautiously she began to pay closer heed to her surroundings. She could hear water sloshing in the bilges and dripping steadily as it leaked through decks and topsides. They must be on the pinnace Hugo had hired to take cargo to London. He'd told her at supper, that evening at Mill Hall, that he'd arranged for it to stop at Maidstone for a cargo of fuller's earth.

"Madam," Jennet whispered again. "Are you awake?"

Susanna rolled toward the sound of her friend's voice. "Speak low," she warned. "Are you still bound?"

"Aye. Hand and foot."

"Are you hurt?"

"Only my pride." There was a hesitation before she spoke again. "And you, madam? You have been most . . . agitated."

"I was drugged." In addition to causing vivid dreams and slowing the heart rate, the mandrake was probably as much to blame for the continued roiling of Susanna's stomach as was her natural tendency toward seasickness. She could only hope she would not suffer any of the other side effects. If she remembered aright, the plant also had emetic and cathartic properties.

"I was conscious when they brought us here from the inn," Jennet said. "They rolled us up in canvas for the journey. Threw us into a cart with other bolts of fabric and had us delivered to quayside and loaded aboard this ship."

"Could you see anything?"

"Not until they unwrapped us." Her tone of voice conveyed her feelings about such treatment. "It felt as if we were carried down two levels and dumped, left in a heap until Mistress Damascin Edgecumbe and Hugo Garrard deigned to inspect their cargo."

"They unwrapped us?"

"Yes. And they had a light. Cargo fills the space all around us. Barrels and chests."

"How long ago did we set sail?" The unquietness in Susanna's stomach increased. She concentrated on Jennet's answer, hoping to distract herself.

"I am not certain. Before they came below."

That meant Damascin and Hugo were still aboard. Susanna frowned. What did they intend?

Still under the influence of the mandrake, Susanna found she had difficulty making sense of anything. When Jennet fell silent, Susanna's mind began to wander. She thought of Nick.

Nick wanted her to go with him to Hamburg. The sweetness of that memory made her smile. Perhaps it would be possible after all. She remembered the story he'd told her about the merchant afraid to leave his house until a crisis forced his hand. She could master her own terror, Susanna told herself, if that was the only way to save her own life and Jennet's. Or she could experiment with the juice of the mandrake, perhaps discover an herbal cure for her panic at the thought of going to sea.

If only mandrake was not as apt to kill as cure.

She did not want to die.

"Madam?"

"Yes, Jennet?"

"I've worked one hand loose."

The announcement snapped Susanna out of a dangerous lethargy. She could not rely on Nick or anyone else to rescue them. By letting her thoughts drift, she'd wasted valuable time lying there, not even trying to escape.

"Excellent, Jennet. See if you can do the same with the other one."

An eternity seemed to pass as Susanna struggled in vain with her own bonds. Then she felt Jennet's fingers, clumsy but determined, tugging at the velvet ropes. A few minutes later, they were both free.

Tentatively Susanna flexed her fingers. Feeling returned in a painful rush, but she welcomed the reminder that she was still alive, still had a chance to get away.

"We've stopped moving," Jennet whispered.

Rubbing the numbness from her feet and ankles,

Susanna considered their situation. Damascin's plan
must be to drown them. If they were thrown, unconscious, into deep water, their bodies weighted down in
some way, it was unlikely they'd ever be found.

Born of necessity, a plan came to her.

Approaching footsteps sounded on the deck above,
then began to descend some sort of ladder.

"Pretend you are still bound and unconscious,"
Susanna whispered to Jennet. "Be ready to follow my
lead, even if my actions seem foolhardy." She hid her
hands behind her back and tucked her ankles up under her skirt.

What was unmistakably Damascin's voice broke the
ensuing silence. "Quickly. Bring them both up on deck
while the crew is distracted."

Susanna felt herself lifted and slung over a bony
shoulder. Hugo, she presumed. He was stronger than
his thin frame suggested. She risked a peek through
her lowered lashes just as he caught Jennet about the
waist and tucked her beneath his other arm. The only
light came from the lantern Damascin held. Fortunately, the shutter was nearly closed. It did not give
off enough illumination to reveal the betraying strips
of velvet Jennet had carelessly left lying in plain sight.

They emerged from the 'tween decks, Hugo stagger-
ing a bit under the combined weight of the two
women, to the boisterous sounds of a celebration.
Whatever the "distraction" Damascin had arranged, it
was taking place behind the closed door of the cap-
tain's cabin.

The deck appeared to be deserted, what little
Susanna could see of it. Night had fallen, a particularly
dark night in the time of the new moon. Damascin's
lantern bobbed ahead, guiding Hugo toward the front
of the vessel.

Susanna braced herself to implement her hastily

made plan, the only means of escape she had been able to devise. She had to act quickly, before their captors noticed that the prisoners were no longer tied hand and foot.

Hugo lowered her onto the wet and clammy deck and deposited Jennet in a limp heap at her side. When he stepped back, turning to speak to Damascin, Susanna flung herself up and over the rail.

"Now, Jennet," she shouted. "Into the river."

There was no time to hesitate, or to panic. In an instant Susanna was free of the ship. Falling. With a mighty splash, water closed over her head. Her heavy skirts clung to her legs, pulling her down, just as they had when she was twelve.

Just as they did in her nightmares.

She fought the memories. Fought the fear. Propelling herself upward, she surfaced in time to hear Jennet enter the water a few yards to her right. Several strong strokes brought Susanna to her friend's side just as Jennet's head popped up again. Sputtering and gasping, Jennet flailed with arms and legs and came close to striking Susanna in the nose.

"Be still!"

Years of obedience had their effect. Jennet stopped struggling.

Susanna grasped her beneath the chin and began to tow her away from the wooden hull. Above them they could hear Damascin's shrill voice and Hugo's deep one, but Susanna felt confident that they would not dare raise an alarm.

Careful to keep Jennet's face out of the water, Susanna increased her speed. The light from the lantern faded away. Only then did it belatedly occur to her that they might have come farther from Maidstone than she'd thought. She'd assumed they were somewhere on the Medway, that swimming a short distance in either direction would bring them to a riverbank. But what if they had reached the Thames estuary at Rochester or beyond? She might be heading out to sea.

A faltering stroke filled her mouth with water. It tasted foul, but not salty. River water.

She swam more strongly, but it was difficult to make much headway when she was weighed down not only by Jennet but by the increasing heaviness of her own skirts.

"Kick your feet, Jennet," she ordered.

Sound carried well over water. An instant after she spoke, another voice responded, but it was not Jennet's. It came from just ahead, and it called out her name.

Susanna went still, scarce daring to believe what she heard.

A dark shape loomed up in front of her. The familiar voice issued from it. "Susanna? Where are you?"

"Nick?"

She still thought she must be imagining things, until the shape drew close enough to resolve itself into a small rowing boat of the sort fishermen used. A pair of sturdy arms reached over the side and took Jennet from her. Nick's fingers gripped Susanna's uplifted hand. A moment later, she was hauled aboard.

He did not let her go.

Held tight in Nick's embrace, Susanna's fears vanished. She was filled with the sheer joy of being alive. Best of all, 'she could see the shore. It was so close at hand that she knew she'd have been able to make it to safety on her own, but she discovered she had no complaints about being rescued.

"How did you get here?" she asked as the boat bumped against the shingle.

"We've been following the pinnace ever since she

set sail from Newhithe. We arrived just after she left quayside. Fortunately for us, the road runs along the shore. When she dropped anchor at dusk, I sent Fulke to find a boat. We were on our way to rescue you when we heard the splash." He paused and she heard the emotion in his voice when he continued. "That was a bad moment, Susanna. We feared we'd come too late."

Nick lifted Susanna out of the boat and carried her the short distance to where Fulke was waiting with the horses. One look at Susanna and Jennet had him scurrying to find something dry to wrap them in. In short order he'd produced a wool cloak and a fustian blanket.

"Take them back to Maidstone," Nick ordered, "while we deal with those aboard the pinnace."

"We'll wait and go back together." Susanna was shivering, but she did not want to leave. Not until this was over.

Nick did not argue, but he made a quick, efficient business of boarding the vessel and taking Hugo and Damascin into custody.

"They were so busy quarreling with each other," he reported a short time later, after they'd brought the prisoners on shore, "that they never noticed us until it was too late."

The small clearing in which they'd gathered to organize the trip back to Maidstone was brightly lit with torches. Susanna took one look at Damascin's face and had to turn away. The woman was nearly incoherent with rage. She hurled invectives at Hugo and tried to cast all the blame on him.

Once again, she misjudged her power over a man.

"Enough!" Hugo bellowed.

In the brief silence that followed, Lionel led Damascin away. This time, she was the one bound hand and foot with velvet ropes.

Hugo turned back to speak to Adrian Ridley as Simon urged him after her, toward the waiting horses. "I will make a full confession," he vowed.

Ridley's somber expression did not change. "That may not be enough to help Lucy. 'Intent to cure' charges may still be made against her. And her faith is still a factor."

Hugo gave a short bark of laughter. "As one who was preparing himself to become a justice of the peace, I can tell you that you have naught to worry about. When the authorities hear from me how they were duped, they'll be too embarrassed to continue to harass one old woman."

As Hugo was marched off under guard, Ridley looked thoughtful. "He may be right. And the scandal of Mistress Damascin's trial and execution should overshadow all else."

"No doubt," Susanna said in a dry voice, "Chediok Norden will write a pamphlet about it."

"Are you ready to go back now?" Nick asked when the two prisoners and their escort had ridden off toward Maidstone.

They had taken all but one of the torches with them, leaving the clearing dimly lit. Even so, Susanna could see that only two horses remained for five people. "We seem to be short of mounts."

"Since I do not imagine your opinion of travel by water has improved in the last few hours, I suggest you ride with me."

What she could manage on water after this experience remained to be seen, but for the present Susanna had to admit that she did prefer to remain on solid ground. Still wrapped in the borrowed cloak, she waited while Nick mounted, then allowed Fulke to lift her onto the saddle in front of him.

"I'd as soon go by boat." Jennet declared when Fulke indicated she'd have to ride double with him.

"She's recovered from her ordeal," Susanna murmured.

In the end, Jennet capitulated. Toby walked ahead with the torch to light the way. As they made their way back to the town, Nick gave Susanna a lively account of Norden's escape and their subsequent search of Damascin's chamber.

"But how did you know we had been taken aboard the pinnace?" Susanna interrupted. "I had forgotten myself that Hugo had hired a ship and arranged for it to come to Maidstone."

By the faint glimmer of torch and starlight, she caught the flash of Nick's teeth as he grinned. "You may have difficulty believing this part of the story. It was my mother who realized you must have been taken out on the Medway."

On top of all the other shocks of the day, this one left her speechless.

"She is well aware that this makes twice she has sent me after you to save your life," Nick continued. "She seems, however, to have become resigned to her fate. In fact, I suspect she plans to go on looking out for your well-being while I am in Hamburg."

The prospect provoked both amusement and horror. As they rode on toward Maidstone, she gave Nick a quick, hard embrace. Little did he realize, she thought, that he might just have presented her with the final bit of incentive she'd been needing to brave the open sea once more.

ABOUT THE AUTHOR

Kathy Lynn Emerson lives in Wilton, Maine. She has written many novels, including romantic suspense and children's mysteries. You can visit her Web site at www.kathylynnemerson.com.

Your Favorite Mystery Authors
Are Now Just A Phone Call Away